Wren Santino was the last person Titus would have ever expected to show up at his house. Finding her in his backyard just after midnight on a late winter night? He couldn't have imagined that if he'd tried.

But she was there.

Pale faced. Bleeding. Handcuffed.

And being shot at.

He pulled his handgun from its chest holster as he army crawled in the direction of the gunfire.

He slid through the shrubs that butted up against the underside of the deck.

"Don't go after them," Wren whispered, so close he knew she had followed silently.

"Them?" he replied.

"Two men dressed in Hidden Cove deputy uniforms. Both are armed. They shot Ryan. I think he's dead. Don't make yourself a target, Titus. Ryan has already been shot. I don't want the same to happen to you."

Aside from her faith and her family, there's not much **Shirlee McCoy** enjoys more than a good book! When she's not hanging out with the people she loves most, she can be found plotting her next Love Inspired Suspense story or trekking through the wilderness, training with a local search-and-rescue team. Shirlee loves to hear from readers. If you have time, drop her a line at shirlee@shirleemccoy.com.

Books by Shirlee McCoy

Love Inspired Suspense

FBI: Special Crimes Unit

Night Stalker
Gone
Dangerous Sanctuary
Lone Witness
Falsely Accused

Mission: Rescue

Protective Instincts
Her Christmas Guardian
Exit Strategy
Deadly Christmas Secrets
Mystery Child
The Christmas Target
Mistaken Identity
Christmas on the Run

Visit the Author Profile page at Harlequin.com for more titles.

FALSELY ACCUSED

SHIRLEE MCCOY

🌿
LOVE INSPIRED SUSPENSE
INSPIRATIONAL ROMANCE

LOVE INSPIRED® SUSPENSE
INSPIRATIONAL ROMANCE

Recycling programs
for this product may
not exist in your area.

ISBN-13: 978-1-335-57439-8

Falsely Accused

Love Inspired
22 Adelaide St. West, 40th Floor
Toronto, Ontario M5H 4E3, Canada
www.Harlequin.com

Printed in U.S.A.

My soul melteth for heaviness:
strengthen thou me according unto thy word.
–Psalm 119:28

To my children. With all my love. Today and always.

ONE

This was wrong. All of it. The squad car speeding along the winding mountain road, heading away from town and deeper into the Maine wilderness. The blood dripping down her arm and onto the leather seat. The silence of the two deputies who had arrested her.

Deputies?

Special Agent Wren Santino wasn't sure about that.

Not anymore.

They hadn't used their police radios. Not to call for medical assistance for her or for the deputy who had been shot. Not to call in a location, call for backup or do as she requested and ask for the FBI Boston Field Office to be contacted.

She might not be an expert on much, but she knew law enforcement protocol, and, after nearly a decade working as a special agent for the FBI, she knew this was going down all wrong.

She shifted in the seat, the scent of leather mixing with the odor of stale vomit and sweat. Blood oozed from the bullet hole in her forearm and snaked around her wrist, sliding under the metal handcuffs. She should be heading to the hospital. Not the town's small sheriff's department. And Ryan? The deputy who had been shot? The closest thing to a brother she'd ever had? They should be life-flighting him to a trauma center.

The thought of him as she'd seen him last—lying in a pool of his own blood—made her even more desperate to escape.

She twisted her uninjured wrist, hoping the seeping blood would make it easy to slip her hand out.

But, of course, that wasn't how cuffs were designed.

She knew that.

The same way she knew that she was in trouble.

She glanced out the back window. Her SUV was a dark smudge against the sepia tones of the forest behind it. She could still see Deputy Ryan Parker's squad car, parked just behind the SUV, pulled a little crookedly onto a grassy area beside the road.

She shouldn't have stopped. Not on a road like this. Not at this time of night. He'd have understood if she'd put on her hazards, slowed her pace and continued driving until she'd reached a less lonely stretch of road. That was the advice she gave students in the women's self-defense classes she taught.

Don't stop if it feels unsafe.

Any legitimate officer will understand.

Hazards on.

Slow your speed.

Keep going until you reach a more populated area.

She hadn't followed her own advice. She'd seen the lights, and she'd pulled over. Maybe because she hadn't expected trouble. Maybe because she was always prepared for it. She hadn't been carrying her service weapon, but she'd had mace in the pocket of her jacket and a repertoire of self-defense tactics that had served her well in the past.

At thirty-six years old, she knew how to defend herself, and how to guard against danger and trouble.

She hadn't thought it would come to her on the lonely stretch of highway between town and the farm belonging to her foster mother, Abigail, but she should have been able to extricate herself from it.

She turned her attention to the two men dressed in Hidden Cove Sheriff's Department uniforms. They looked legit. The jackets. The badges. The shirts and hats that were pulled low over their eyes. Clean-shaven. Caucasian. One with fair skin. One with an olive complexion. The fact that she could see those things meant they weren't trying to hide their identities. She wanted to believe that was a good thing, but her gut was telling her something different.

No legitimate law enforcement officer left a man lying on the ground bleeding.

"What about Deputy Parker? You can't just leave him there. He needs medical attention," she said, trying to engage them in a conversation that went beyond the Miranda rights they'd read her before they'd cuffed her and shoved her in the back of their squad car.

"You probably should have thought about that before you shot him," the driver said. Mid-to late-twenties. Slim build. A small scar on his jaw. His hair was hidden, but Wren would guess it to be dark to match his tan skin.

"I already told you, I didn't shoot him. The shots were fired just before you arrived." Ryan had pulled her over. She'd realized it was him after he'd gotten out of his squad car. He'd told her that he was in trouble and that he needed her help. She'd stepped out of the SUV. Before he could explain more, a shot had been fired, and he'd gone down. She'd reached for his service weapon and had been shot while trying to free it.

Not a kill-shot.

Not like the one that had taken Ryan down.

She swallowed a wave of grief. Like Wren, Ryan had been one of Abigail's foster kids. A teenager with no future who'd been shuffled through too many placements for too long, he'd arrived at the farm three years after Wren. It had taken a while, but eventually they'd warmed up to one another. By the time she'd left for college, she'd thought of him as her annoying kid brother—still finding trouble, still not settled into the structured life Abigail offered. She had been frustrated with his lack of progress, but she had also been hopeful that he would grow up and mature.

Still, she had been surprised when he'd told her he planned to become a police officer. She'd been even more surprised when he had decided to stay in Hidden Cove. Small-town life wasn't anything either of them had been used to when they'd arrived. Both had often complained about the constraints of living in a town where everyone knew everyone else's business. As a teen, Ryan had always been chomping at the bit, ready to break free of the life he had been forced into. The idea of him getting a job with the local police and staying in Hidden Cove hadn't been on Wren's radar.

But then, she had never been close to Ryan.

She'd loved him like a brother, but they had been too far apart in age and in personality to be friends. The inner workings of his mind had always been as mysterious to her as hers had been to him.

Now, he was gone, and she was being

questioned about his murder as if she were a suspect or the perpetrator.

"I didn't have anything to do with the shooting. Swab my hands for gun residue, take me in for questioning, but while you're doing all that, make sure you have someone out there looking for the real perpetrator," she said, hoping to illicit a response from one of the men.

They remained silent. No further comment on her supposed shooting of a man she considered a brother, no questions asked in the hope of getting answers that could be used against her. The silence in the vehicle was eerie. The space between her and the two officers was unencumbered by mesh or Plexiglas.

This wasn't like any police cruiser she had ever been in. There were locks and handles on the interior door panels. Easy escape for a criminal who wanted to get away. As far as she had been able to see, there wasn't a radio or computer attached to the console. Even a low-budget, low-tech police department would have radios in the vehicles.

She shifted forward to get a better look, and the fairer-skinned man lifted a gun and aimed it in her direction.

"Back off," he said harshly, barely glancing in her direction.

She did. She'd already seen what she wanted to. She had been correct. There was no police radio in the car. No computer system. Nothing tying this vehicle to the sheriff's department. If these men were imposters, they had to be tied to Ryan's shooting. If that were the case, they had an agenda that didn't include taking her to the sheriff's department and booking her on federal charges. This area of Maine was largely unpopulated, deep forest and stretching across the landscape. It would be easy to get rid of a body here— to hide someone and make it seem as if that person had gone on the run.

What kind of trouble were you in, Ryan? she silently asked. Something big. So big he had been killed because of it, and it looked as if Wren was being set up to be the fall guy. If she didn't escape, her SUV and Ryan's squad car would eventually be found. His body would be discovered, and she would be gone—a story people told for years to come. How an FBI agent killed her foster brother and then went on the lam. The police would be searching for her instead of searching for the real killer, but she would never be found. Her body would be buried somewhere deep in the Maine wilderness.

And that was something she couldn't allow.

Not just because she was innocent and needed to prove it, but because she wanted justice for Ryan. She wanted the person who had shot him to be punished to the full extent of the law. She had gone into law enforcement to make that happen to as many criminals as she could. She had committed herself to that goal, and she had spent more than a decade of her life devoted to it. Everything she was, all that she did, was tied up in her need to see justice served. She had no regrets about that.

Lately, though, she had been tired.

She had returned home after long days of work at the FBI's Boston field office and asked herself if her devotion to justice was worth the silent and empty apartment, the lack of romantic relationships, the bonds of friendship that had become frayed and worn after years of missed and rescheduled get-togethers. Returning to Hidden Cove to help Abigail had seemed like the perfect opportunity to reassess her life and her goals. Wren had imagined plenty of downtime spent walking the farm or hiking through the woods.

She hadn't imagined this.

She hadn't anticipated it.

She was neck-deep in trouble, and she was the only person who could get herself out of it.

She slid sideways on the seat, watching as the vehicle zipped past shadowy trees.

She knew this road well and knew exactly where she was. She'd traveled this way hundreds of times as a preteen and teenager. She knew the curves and the hills, the places where it opened up and where it narrowed.

She knew that the next turnoff led down a long dirt driveway to a tired-looking bungalow-style house that overlooked Mystic Creek. She thought the place had been abandoned years ago, but she wasn't sure. She hadn't asked Abigail, because she hadn't wanted her to know that there were still times when she thought about the bungalow and about Titus Anderson. Even after all these years.

She watched as the driver flew past the old white mailbox that marked the Anderson property. They were going too fast for the road, taking curves too quickly, tree branches scraping the sides and roof of the vehicle. If she jumped out now, she could be too badly injured to run.

She waited, her arm still seeping blood, her attention focused.

They traveled another couple of miles, and then the driver braked hard, spinning onto a side road, the car slowing just enough that she was willing to take the chance. *Had* to take it, because it might be the only one she got.

She opened the door and threw herself out, trying to jump clear of the back wheels. Her shoulder slammed into the thick trunk of a pine tree, needles jabbing her face as she stumbled and tried to regain her balance.

She fell, her forehead glancing off the rough bark, knees sliding across dead leaves and aromatic needles. The screech of brakes spurred her up and on.

Faster.

Faster.

The word chanted through her mind, her pulse matching the frantic rhythm of it. She was making too much noise, giving away her location with every frantic push forward.

She needed to slow down, be quiet, think through her options, because if she didn't, she'd die. And, in a place like this, it might be years before she was found.

If she ever was.

And maybe that was what this was about. The trouble Ryan was in had led to his murder, and she was slated to be the fall-guy for it. All the perps had to do was get her away from the murder scene, kill her and hide her body where no one would ever find it. With her vehicle left near Ryan's body, she could be pinned with the crime and called a fugitive from justice. She wasn't going to let that happen.

She forced herself to stop and listen.

They were behind her, crashing through the thick undergrowth, breaking branches and twigs. They'd have lights. She was certain of that. She didn't glance back to see if she was right. She turned to her left, walking parallel to the road rather than away from it. Moving deliberately, being careful where she stepped and what she bumped. The moon was high and bright. It had been rising when she'd left the rehabilitation center where Abigail had been staying since she'd broken her hip. Now, it had reached its zenith and was descending. She used it as a guide. East would lead her back to the dirt driveway and Titus's childhood home. His mother had died when they were in college, overdosing on the drugs that had stolen her away from him years prior to her death. He'd inherited the house, but he'd told her that he never planned to return to it.

They'd still been best friends then.

Now they were strangers, but she knew how to find her way through the woods and to his childhood home. She knew that the back door didn't lock properly, that there was a rotary phone hanging on the kitchen wall, that an old Chevy truck sat in the garage near the back of the property.

At least, those things had been true

when she'd left town eighteen years ago. Maybe they were still true. Maybe she could walk in the back door, grab the phone and dial 911. She knew enough about Titus to know he wouldn't have let the property go to waste. He would have rented it out or sold it, and he would have made certain the electricity, water and phone were always on. There had been too many times during his childhood when they hadn't been.

So, the phone would be working.

It had to be.

And the place would either belong to someone else or be a rental property managed by Titus.

Either way, she should be able to find the help she needed.

She hoped.

Staying in the woods, trying to keep a step ahead of her pursuers when she was cuffed and injured would be a death sentence.

She shuddered, her body suddenly cold with shock.

Ryan was dead.

The reality of it seemed to finally be sinking in, and she was sick from it. Her stomach churned, her head pounded, her feet felt numb. She stumbled down a steep slope, falling face-first into a small creek. Cold water filled her mouth and nose, nearly choking her. She refused to cough, afraid her pursuers would hear. *She* could hear *them* shoving through the trees, closer than she wanted them to be. They hadn't been fooled by her change in direction. They were hot on her trail, and if she didn't do something quickly they'd find her.

She struggled to her feet, slipped and slid up the opposite side of the bank, praying for help, wondering if it would come. She wanted to run, but her legs were heavy, her body shaking with the force of her heartbeat. She had to settle for slow, steady progress. Down a hill and up the other side, the sound of her pursuers echoing through the otherwise silent woods.

From the sound of it, they were racing toward her, sprinting through the early spring foliage.

She needed to run, too, but she could barely manage to walk. A light flashed through the trees. She thought the men had circled around and were setting a trap, but the light remained steady as she ducked behind an ancient oak. Her heart jumped as she realized what she was seeing. Not the beam of a flashlight. A house light. She ran as fast as she dared. Finally breaking free of the forest and sprinting across lush grass. Her harsh breath was the only sound in eerily quiet darkness. The house was a few hundred yards away—a little bungalow that looked like a sweeter, more-cared-for version of the one Titus had once lived in. Manicured yard and whitewashed porch with a swing hanging from its ceiling. The light she'd been aiming for shone from a front window. Another was visible in the attic dormer.

A man cursed, the sound breaking the

silence. Seconds later, she heard the soft click of a gun safety. She dove for cover, sliding across grass as the first bullet flew. It slammed into the earth inches away, kicking up bits of rock and damp soil. She managed to roll behind a bush and shimmy a few feet closer to the house, blood oozing in thick warm rivulets down her wrist and seeping into the back of her shirt and the waistband of her jeans.

She kept low as another bullet hit the ground.

She was almost to safety, crawling across the ground on her belly, her toes and knees propelling her forward, her pulse slushing loudly in her ears and blocking every other sound. She had no idea if her pursuers were approaching, no clue whether they'd fled. She knew only her goal: to escape, to survive, to get help for herself and justice for Ryan.

She skirted the front of the house and crawled around the corner, out of the line of fire. She managed to get to her feet again, to run the length of the house and around to the back. The door was there, just like she remembered it. Three steps up. Grab the doorknob. Turn it. That's all she had to do. She made it up the stairs, managed to turn her back to the door and grab the knob with her cuffed hand.

Only, instead of opening like it had when she was a kid, it remained closed, the lock holding.

She tried again, afraid to knock and give away her location. When it didn't open, she searched the back porch for a spare key. The beam of a flashlight skipped across the yard near the corner of the house, and she darted down the steps, tried to run to the back of the property.

Too late.

Someone grabbed her shoulder, hard fingers digging into tense muscles. She whirled, sideswiping her attacker's ankle. He swayed but didn't fall. She shoved forward, using her body weight against him, trying to knock him to the ground. He muttered something, his grip loosening almost enough for her to break free.

She tried again. This time he stepped sideways, letting her tumble to the ground. She fell hard, the breath knocked from her lungs, her vision blurring. She could have stayed down, but she'd been fighting hard battles most of her life, and all she really knew was how to keep going.

She managed to roll to her back and was struggling to get up when a bullet whizzed past and slammed into a deck railing. Wood splintered, a piece of it digging into her cheek. She had no time to react.

Her attacker was on her, pressing her into the cool grass. All her training flew out of her head. All the years of careful control were gone. In an instant, she was back in time, fighting off the man who had just murdered her mother. She brought her knee up. Or tried. He had her pinned. Legs pressed to legs, chest to chest, his entire body covering hers.

She twisted, the bone in her injured arm snapping. She would have passed out if adrenaline hadn't been pouring through her. She bucked, trying to throw off his weight.

"Stop!" he growled. "Someone's shooting at you, and we're both in the crosshairs. I don't know what your plans are for tonight, but I'm not planning to die."

It was the voice rather than the words that stilled her frantic movements. She knew the gritty texture of it, the soft Southern drawl that had never left. Not even a decade after moving to Hidden Cove with his mother.

"Titus?" she managed to say, the name ringing hollowly in her ears.

He tensed, then shifted just enough so she could breathe.

"Wren?" he responded.

He was looking into her face, staring into her eyes like he had dozens of times when they were kids exploring the woods together.

"What's going—?"

Another bullet slammed into the deck, and his weight pressed into her again. This time, though, she didn't fight it. She hadn't been thinking clearly when she'd headed toward his property. If she had she wouldn't have done it. Bringing danger into someone else's life wasn't the way she operated. She didn't want Titus hurt because of her, and if she could have jumped up and led the gunmen away, she would have.

"You need to get out of here," she whispered.

"We need to get out of here," he responded, his lips brushing her ear. "Who is it? What does he want?"

"I don't know who he is. What he wants is me dead," she replied.

"How about we don't let him achieve his goal? Stay down and stay quiet. I'll see if I can get a visual." He rolled away, cold air replacing the warmth of his body as he moved.

She wanted to tell him not to go. She wanted to remind him that she was an FBI agent and knew how to take care of herself and her problems, but her thoughts were sluggish. Before the words could form, he was gone, disappearing like a wraith into the darkness.

Wren Santino was the last person Titus would have ever expected to show up at his house. Finding her in his backyard just after midnight on a late winter night? He couldn't have imagined that if he'd tried.

But she was there.

Pale faced. Bleeding. Handcuffed.

And being shot at.

It had been years since they had last spoken to each other. That had been his fault. It was a fact he had acknowledged each time he had been tempted to reach for the phone to call her or make the trip to Boston to visit. Selfishly, he had wanted absolution and a return of the companionship and friendship he had lost. But, he had known Wren well enough to know that if she wanted to offer any of those things, she would have reached out to him.

She never had.

Until now.

He pulled his handgun from its chest holster as he army crawled in the direction of the gunfire. He knew he had to stop the shooter, but he hated leaving Wren alone. They had been best friends. Buddies. Confidantes. She'd stood as his best man when he'd married Meghan.

He knew her almost as well as he knew himself, and he didn't trust her to stay where he had left her. Even injured and cuffed, she would try to apprehend the shooter. He glanced back but couldn't see her through the darkness. He couldn't hear her, either, and he took that as a good sign.

He slid through the shrubs that butted up against the underside of the deck. He'd been meaning to dig them up. Now he was glad he hadn't. He waited a few seconds, listening to the sudden silence, watching the darkness beyond the manicured yard.

"Don't go after them," Wren whispered, so close he knew she had followed silently.

"Them?" he replied, glancing back and meeting her dark eyes. She was on her stomach, her skin pasty white in the gloom.

"Two men dressed in Hidden Cove deputy uniforms. Both are armed."

"You're sure they aren't actually police?" he asked.

"They shot Ryan. I think he's dead, but I'm not sure. It's possible that he can be saved if help arrives soon enough. I'd rather have you call for an ambulance than run into the woods looking for the shooters."

"Your Ryan?" Titus asked, knowing that it had to be, that there was only one Ryan in town who Wren was affiliated with.

"Yes." Her voice broke, and he had to resist the urge to hug her the way he would

have before he'd ruined everything between them.

"I've already called 911. Help should be
here soon, but letting them go? That's not
going to work for me." He'd noticed the
blood trail in his front yard as soon as
he'd walked outside. He'd thought it might
be an animal wounded by a hunter who
was shooting out of season and on private
property. That had made the most sense to
him. He'd been back in Hidden Cove for
four years. He'd found more than a couple
poachers on his property.

Usually he let them go with a warning.

Tonight, he had been in the mood to
press charges.

He had called 911 and then he'd gone
out to look for the perpetrator. He hadn't
expected to be shot at, but he had been
prepared for almost anything.

"Don't make yourself a target, Titus,"
Wren said. "Ryan has already been shot.
I don't want the same to happen to you."

"Where is he?"

"Near his cruiser. About five miles outside of town. On Mountain Road. My SUV is there. The police shouldn't have any trouble finding him."

The faint sound of sirens drifted on the breeze. "It sounds like help is almost here," she said.

"Wait for them here. I'll be back as soon as I can," he said, crawling away, army-style.

"You're not going to find the shooters. They're heading back to their vehicle. There's no way they're going to wait around for the police to arrive," she said, shifting into a sitting position.

"Get down," he barked, fear making his tone harsher than he'd intended.

"I need to get these cuffs off, and I need to get back to my SUV. My cell phone is there. I want to call the FBI Boston Field Office and get some of my colleagues up here."

"Wren, get down," he repeated, crossing the distance between them.

"You don't have any handcuff keys, do

you?" she asked, dark strands of hair sliding across her cheek as she tried to get to her feet.

"I stopped carrying those when I quit the Boston Police Department," he responded.

"I have some in my SUV."

"I guess you have a good reason for that?"

"Yeah. You never know when you might need them." She didn't smile, but there was some life in her eyes again. "I want these guys. Sitting in cuffs while they escape isn't helping me get them. You have a car?"

"Yes."

"Good. Let's go." She strode toward the two-story garage as if she knew he would only ever park his Jeep there. Because, of course, he did. Jeep in the garage. Coats in the closet. Keys on the hook by the front door. Everything in its place. All of it in order and neat.

She knew that. She knew him. More than most people.

His hang-ups and his habits.

And she had loved him anyway. The way one friend loves another. That had meant the world to him.

It still did.

He followed, making another call to 911 as he unlocked the garage and flicked on the light. He had the keys and his cell phone in his pocket. He unlocked the Jeep, helped Wren into the passenger seat, his hand curved around her biceps.

She'd always been muscular and fit. Now she felt fragile, her tendons and ligaments drawn tight over small bones. He reached for the seat belt.

"Don't worry about that," she said.

He shook his head. "Safety first."

She didn't argue. He had known she wouldn't.

He knew her. Just like she knew him.

He climbed into the driver's seat and started the engine, pulling out of the garage and onto the dirt driveway that led to Mountain Road. They bounced over the deep ruts that he planned to fill when the weather warmed up and then turned onto the paved road that led to town.

She'd said Ryan was there.

Ambushed by the men who'd been trying to kill her.

He was thinking about that, watching the road in front of him more than he was the road behind. He expected to see emergency vehicles speeding toward his place. When he glanced in his rearview mirror and saw a car coming up fast behind him, it took him by surprise. No headlights. Just white paint gleaming in the moonlight.

"What's wrong?" Wren asked, shifting to look out the back window. "That's them," she murmured, her voice cold with anger or fear.

"Good. Let's see if we can lead them to the police."

"They'll run us off the road before then."

Probably, but the closer they were to help when it happened, the better off they'd be. He sped around a curve in the road, the white car closing the gap between them. It tapped his bumper, knocking the Jeep sideways. He straightened, steering the Jeep back onto the road, and tried to accelerate into the next curve as he was rear-ended again.

This time, the force of the impact sent him spinning out of control. The Jeep glanced off a guardrail, bounced back onto the road and then off it, tumbling down into a creek and landing nose down in the soft creek bed.

He didn't have time to think about damage, to ask if Wren was okay or to make another call to 911. He knew the men in the car were going to come for them.

Come for *Wren*.

And he was going to make certain they didn't get her.

He unsnapped his seat belt and jumped out of the vehicle.

"What are you doing?" Wren asked, her hands behind her, unable to do anything to free herself. He reached across the seat and unsnapped her belt.

"I'm going to discourage them from coming down here to find you," he said, backing out of the Jeep.

"It will be easier and less dangerous to let them come to us," she replied, scooting across the center console and climbing out.

"Only if you stay out of sight and let me handle it," he replied.

"What's that supposed to mean?"

"It means, they're after you. If you walk to them, they're going to get exactly what they're hoping for."

"I'm not going to wait here while you fight my battles," she argued.

"You have no idea whose battle this is. Neither do I. But right now? We're both in danger. Since I'm currently the only one capable of fighting, I'll do it for both of us. You can have your turn next time.

Get back in the Jeep. I'll return as soon as I can."

She raised a dark brow, but did as he asked, sitting in the driver's seat as he turned toward the road. He pulled his gun from the holster, keeping it ready as he began the steep ascent. He had quit law enforcement a few years after he had found out the truth about Meghan. It wasn't something he had planned or, even, contemplated. Being a Boston cop had been his life goal. He had achieved it and had enjoyed moving up in ranks, becoming a homicide detective and following the path he had planned for himself.

But, when the opportunity to quit and change careers had presented itself, he hadn't hesitated. He'd dived in headfirst and prayed it would work out. Four years after he'd returned to Hidden Cove and taken over his old carpentry teacher's restoration business, he finally felt like he'd found his niche, but he hadn't forgotten what it was like to be a police officer. He

knew how to pursue suspects and apprehend perpetrators. He wasn't going to
allow the men who had run him off the
road to escape. There was too much riding on their being apprehended. Justice.
The safety of the community.

And, most importantly, Wren's safety.

It may have been years since they'd last
spoken, but he still cared about her, and
he wasn't going to step back and allow her
to be hurt by an unknown enemy.

A door slammed, and he stopped,
crouching behind thick undergrowth as he
waited for the perps to make their move.

TWO

Nine years was a long time to not speak to the best of friends, the staunchest supporter, the most enthusiastic encourager.

Nine years should have changed everything, but the rhythm of her friendship with Titus? It was the same. The verbal sparring. The quick exchanges of ideas and plans. The compromising and the challenging. It all felt as natural as breathing.

That was the only excuse Wren could find for allowing him to walk toward the perpetrators while she sat in the Jeep and waited.

His plan had made sense.

He'd presented his argument, and she'd agreed because he'd been right. She wasn't in the position to win a skirmish let alone the battle she thought might be coming.

But sitting idle?

It wasn't something she did well.

She scooted closer to the door, legs out of the Jeep, feet on the muddy ground. Her tennis shoes were already soaked through, the cuffs of her jeans damp. If she'd had use of her hands, she'd have rolled them up, removed her shoes and climbed the steep hill that led to the road. She'd done it dozens of times as a teen, returning home with dirty feet and mud-caked clothes and listening to Abigail's good-humored grumbling about her tomboyish ways.

Sirens screamed, the sound echoing through the forest and pulsing behind her eyes. She'd been exhausted before this, pulled in too many directions by too many people. Work. Friends. Abigail. She'd hoped that the two weeks she'd taken off to help her foster mother move her belongings into the retirement home she planned to move into when she was released from rehab would clear her mind and renew her flagging spirit. She hadn't expected this kind of trouble. Not in a place like Hidden Cove.

But she should have been prepared for it.

A year ago, she would have been.

Life had been wearing her down. Fatigue had caused her to make a rookie mistake. Instead of carrying her service revolver, she'd left it in the gun safe at Abigail's. Ryan might have paid for her mistake with his life.

Might have?

No matter how much she kept trying to deny it, she knew the truth.

She blinked back hot tears. Crying did no good. What she needed was razor-sharp focus because she planned to catch his killers, and she planned to throw them in jail and toss away the key.

An engine revved. A door slammed.

She expected a volley of shots to be fired.

Expected to have to duck for cover and worry that Titus was in the line of fire.

He'd quit the Boston Police Department several years after she'd joined the FBI. She'd heard it through the law enforcement grapevine. She'd wanted to call and ask him why. He'd been a great cop and a fantastic homicide detective. He'd been on his way to a great and fulfilling career.

But by the time she'd heard he'd quit, the silence between them had seemed too deep, the distance too great to overcome.

She wondered what he'd been doing since he'd left the force. He still acted like a cop. Still moved like one. She could see him crouched behind brush halfway up the hill, gun in hand and at the ready.

She wanted to call out and tell him to be careful, but that would bring bullets flying in her direction.

Or maybe not.

The car sped away. Lights still off.

She stepped out of the Jeep.

"Stay where you are!" Titus shouted, and she realized she'd made another mistake. She'd assumed both perps had left the area. One might have stayed behind.

She froze, waiting for gunshots.

All she heard was the pulsing siren of the approaching emergency vehicle and the rapid beat of her heart.

"It's clear, I think," she finally responded, stepping out of the muddy creek bed.

"I'd rather we both *know*," he muttered, jogging toward her.

Strobe lights flashed on the street above them.

Help had finally arrived.

She wanted to feel relieved and victorious, but all she felt was grief. Ryan was gone. They hadn't ever been close, but they'd always had each other's backs. She'd bailed him out of jail when he was a young punk kid with more attitude than brains. She'd helped him with college expenses, encouraged him to keep his nose clean and lectured him when he'd needed it.

He'd always called her on her birthday and on holidays. Always sent funny cards reminding her not to take life too seriously. Always called her "sis."

"You okay?" Titus asked as he reached her side.

"Do I look it?" she responded.

His gaze dropped from her face to her blood-splattered T-shirt.

"No." He shrugged out of his flannel shirt and dropped it around her shoulders. "It's going to be okay. We're going to find the person who did this."

"People," she corrected. "Two men."

"We'll find the people who did this. But, first, I need to get you out of these cuffs." He touched her uninjured wrist. "This one is fine, but the other one is so swollen, the cuff is digging in. Can you feel it?"

"It hurts," she responded, her gaze on the road and the flashing lights. "I need to speak with the police."

She headed uphill, her feet slipping, her arms useless for balance.

"How about I help?" Titus muttered,

sliding his arm around her waist, careful not to jar her injured wrist.

If it had been any other day, if he'd been any other man, she'd have told him she could manage on her own, because she *could* manage. She hadn't gotten where she was in her career by relying on other people to get her through the tough times. It might take more time and more effort, but if she'd had to, she'd have crawled to the road.

However, Titus was an old friend. They'd parted ways under unhappy circumstances, but she still cared about him. She'd like to believe he still cared about her. For right now, she *would* believe it, because as much as she hated to admit it, she felt too weak to climb the hill on her own.

They were nearly to the top when a uniformed officer stepped into sight, the beam of his light illuminating them. "Sheriff's department! Freeze! Both of you! Hands where I can see them!"

"Her hands are cuffed," Titus responded.

"Facedown! On your bellies. Now!"

Titus tried to help her, but the deputy shouted again. "I said get down! Now."

Titus dropped to his stomach.

She did the same, her eyes tearing as the sudden movement jarred her injured wrist.

Seconds later, they were surrounded. She counted shoes as she was patted down. Five sets. That was a lot of manpower for a small-town sheriff's department to send out.

"Wren Santino?" one of the men said, grabbing her arm and yanking her to her feet.

"That's correct," she said as she met Sheriff Camden Wilson's eyes. They'd attended high school together. He knew exactly who she was.

"You're under arrest for the murder of Ryan Parker. You have the right to remain silent…"

His voice droned on, but she didn't hear what he was saying.

All she could hear was the word *murder* and Ryan's name.

Ryan was gone. Somehow, she'd been responsible for that.

She was dizzy with the truth of it, and she stumbled, dropping to her knees despite the sheriff's grip on her arm.

"She needs medical attention," Titus said, his voice gruff with concern. She wanted to tell him that she'd be fine, but the words seemed trapped in her head.

"She needs to be in jail for the rest of her life," the sheriff said, but he put in a call for an ambulance. She heard that. Heard the soft murmur of voices as other law enforcement officers chatted.

The sheriff led her to his vehicle. When they reached it, he uncuffed her wrists with more gentleness than she'd expected.

"Thanks," she managed to say.

"You're a human being. You deserve to be treated like one. I wished you'd felt the same about my deputy. Sit." He opened the door and motioned for her to sit in the back.

She didn't argue, and she didn't try to explain.

Her Miranda rights had been read.

She knew them.

"I'd like to make a phone call," she said.

"Later," he replied, and then he closed the door, locking her inside. She'd wait patiently. She'd do what she was told. Fighting the system could only lead to more trouble in the long run, but what she really wanted to do was shout for him to let her out, demand that she be treated like the law enforcement officer she was, give him all the details he had yet to ask for.

She had done nothing wrong.

She knew that.

The best thing she could do was the most difficult— be quiet and wait.

Six hours after he'd been cuffed and taken to the sheriff's department, Titus finally returned home. His Jeep had been towed from the creek and was sitting in front of his house. The windows were shattered and the body damaged. He thought the front axle might be broken. It wasn't drivable, but it wasn't his only vehicle. Despite asking about Wren numerous times, he'd been given no information. Now that he was free, he planned to take matters into his own hands. He'd drive back into town and ask around. Someone knew something about where Wren had been taken and how she was doing.

More than likely, everyone knew everything.

That's how it worked in Hidden Cove.

He'd moved there as a child, making the long trip from Fort Worth, Texas, because his mother had inherited property from her maternal grandfather. By all rights, the home should have been exactly what they'd been needing, but Sophia Parker had been more interested in her addictions than she had been in keeping up the pretty little house and beautiful acreage.

He'd spent his tween and teen years ignoring the whispers about his home life, about his mother's ways of making a few bucks, about his threadbare clothes and wild Afro. He hadn't cared that he was the only dark-skinned kid in town. He'd cared that he'd had to carry his clothes to the Laundromat if he wanted them clean. He cared that he had to buy food if he wanted to eat. He cared that the entire town knew his business.

Now, though, the nosy neighbors and small-town gossips might come in handy.

He ran to the garage and climbed in the Chevy pickup he used to haul wood. It was ancient but functional, the engine roaring to life as soon as he turned the ignition. His gun had been taken and then returned. He had it tucked into the holster, and he grabbed a jacket from his emergency pack in the back of the truck and shrugged into it. No sense wandering around town with his gun visible. People in Hidden Cove hadn't trusted him when he was a kid. He had been an outsider with an attitude, a teenager who had no under-standing of small-town life. His mother's drug addiction had been well known, and he had been her son—a young man who had a chip on his shoulder and no reason to want to fit in.

It had taken a while, but eventually he had proven that he was more than a prod-uct of his mother's mistakes. His job as a police officer in Boston had helped so-lidify the town's impression of him as hardworking and honest. When he had returned for his high school carpen-try teacher's retirement party and had been given an opportunity to take over his restoration business, he had jumped at the opportunity. He had worked with his teacher for two years before stepping in as owner and operator. The town had seemed happy enough with the transition, but Wren had left town to go to college, and she had only returned for brief vis-its. Unlike Titus, she was still considered

an outsider. The fact that she was an FBI
agent might make people more willing to
trust her, but whether or not she'd have
any allies in a town that was close-knit
and tight-lipped when it wanted to be remained to be seen. She did have Abigail,
though, and Abigail had a lot of influence in Hidden Cove. She'd been born and
raised there. She'd taught elementary and
middle school. She'd fostered kids who'd
had nowhere else to go. Never married,
she'd devoted her life to helping others
and supporting the town she loved.

The town loved her for it.

Although he hadn't been to see her at
the farm since his return, they'd spoken at
church and at town meetings. She'd sup-
ported his efforts to save some of the old-
est homes in town, and he'd appreciated
that. She'd broken her hip a month ago,
and, according to people who supposedly
knew, she planned to move into a retirement home once she finished rehab.

The fact that she was giving up the property that had been in her family for three generation made his stomach churn, but it wasn't his business, and when he'd heard that the for-sale sign had finally gone up, he'd kept his mouth shut and his opinions to himself.

Abigail would be devastated when she heard the news about Ryan. She'd loved him like a son. Her two last foster children had been her two best. That's what she'd often said when he was visiting Wren at the farm during their high school years.

He glanced in his rearview mirror as he pulled onto Mountain Road. It had been too long since he'd been out to Abigail's property. He should have visited before she'd broken her hip, but he'd been avoiding the memories he knew it would stir up.

He'd made a lot of mistakes in his life.

Accusing Wren of lying about his ex-wife? That had been one of the biggest. He'd known her almost as well as he knew himself. He'd known how honest she was, how much she cared about him, how deeply it had hurt her to have to tell him she had seen Meghan with another man.

Yet, he'd been more willing to believe she was lying than he had been to accept the truth.

He'd tried to apologize, but by that point it had been too late. The damage had been done.

"Water under the bridge," he muttered, accelerating as he headed toward town. The sun had just risen, golden rays of light tipping the tree canopy with gold. The sky was pristine blue. No clouds, but he caught a whiff of something in the air.

Smoke?

He rolled down the window, inhaled fresh cool air and the unmistakable scent of a fire. He glanced in his rearview mirror, saw black smoke billowing up from the valley.

Surprised, he turned the truck around and sped toward the plume of smoke. It was too big to be coming from a trash pile. Was someone's house burning? He called 911 but, without an address, could only be vague about the location. The road wound its way down into the valley, the forests opening into farmland. He drove several miles, his attention on the road and the smoke wafting across the sky. It took him too long to realize where it was coming from, and by the time he did, he was almost at the gates that opened onto Abigail's two-hundred-acre property. The old farmhouse stood on a hill in the center of a lush green lawn. Gray siding. White shutters. Wraparound porch.

The smoke was coming from behind the house.

Or from the back of it.

He drove through the open gates, speeding up the gravel driveway and giving the address to the 911 operator as he parked. If he didn't do something, the two-hundred-year-old farmhouse would be consumed by flames before help arrived.

He raced to the backyard, hoping an outbuilding or trash pile was on fire. Flames shot from the roof of the kitchen addition that had been added in the fifties. Abigail loved to tell the story of how her father had surprised her mother with the extraordinary gift of a modern kitchen. In the years since, nothing had been changed. The subway-tile backsplash, the Formica counters and glossy pink cupboards were all exactly as they had been. The oven, the refrigerator, the old icebox. They stood exactly where Abigail's father had placed them.

He bounded up the porch stairs. The back door was open, the room beyond filled with smoke. He could see flames lapping at the floor and moving toward the dining room, which was part of the older building.

All the aged and dry wood would be kindling for the inferno. He grabbed the garden hose that Abigail used to water the flower beds and turned on the water.

It wasn't much, but if he could wet down the wood, he might be able to slow the fire.

He aimed for the interior of the kitchen, listening as the fire hissed and steamed, moving into the room as the flames diminished.

There was a trail of liquid on the floor, and the flames followed it, shooting along through the pool of what had to be accelerant.

He aimed at that, spraying water across the floor and into the dining room, skirting past smoldering floorboards and making his way deeper into the house.

He could smell it now—gasoline.

And he could see it, splattered on walls and on the floor, just waiting for the spark to get it going.

Someone had been trying to burn down the farmhouse.

Who?

Why?

And what did it have to do with Ryan's death?

Titus didn't believe in coincidences, and

he didn't believe the two things weren't connected.

He sprayed the floorboards, stretching the hose as far as it could go. Once he'd reached its limits, he headed back into the kitchen. The flames were out there, smothered by the deluge of water, but the damage was massive. He doubted the addition could be saved, but the fire marshal would make that determination.

He caught movement in his periphery vision and turned as a figure lunged from the doorway that led to the back stairs. Something glanced off his head, the pain less immediate than his need to stop his attacker from escaping.

He dropped the hose and tackled what looked like a scrawny teenager. They fell into a puddle of gasoline-tainted water. Titus had the kid pinned, his forearm to the boy's throat.

"Let me go!" the kid whined.

"Not until the police arrive."

"Police? I was trying to put the fire out!"

"You can tell them all about it," Titus said.

The kid's gaze shifted. Just a little. Just enough that Titus had a millisecond of warning. He dove to the side as something whipped through the air. It hit his shoulder, the impact stealing the breath from his lungs.

Not a bullet. He rolled sideways, pulling his gun, aiming at a man who was swinging a baseball bat in the direction of his head. The shot hit its mark, but momentum kept the bat spinning through the air. It hit Titus in the temple.

He saw stars.

Then he saw nothing at all.

THREE

Black smoke rose from the back of Abigail's farmhouse, the dark streaks of soot-filled heat drifting into the sky. No flames that Wren could see, but that didn't make the situation better. Something was burning. The house or the porch behind it. Not an outbuilding. The smoke was too close.

"What in the world?" Annalise Rivers muttered as she pulled up in front of the house. One of the FBI's top-notch defense attorneys, Annalise had arrived at the hospital two hours after Wren had called the field office and requested help. She'd brought Special Agent Radley Tumberg with her. A member of the Special Crimes Unit, Radley had been part of Wren's work world for years. Determined and tough, he knew how to go after the answers he needed to solve some of the most complicated crimes.

Any other time Wren would have found comfort in having him there. Right now, all she felt was confusion, grief and anger.

"Call the fire department!" she shouted as she jumped out of the vehicle, the soft cast the hospital had set her wrist in banging against her chest as the sling bounced with her movement. She'd had the bullet wound cleaned and stitched and the bone set. Until the stitches came out, her arm would remain in the soft cast. She had been released from the hospital with instructions to keep the arm elevated and to rest.

She had planned to go to the rehab center, explain to Abigail what had happened and then return to the farmhouse. Instead, she'd received a call from a nurse at the rehab center. The sheriff had broken the news of Ryan's death, and Abigail was distraught, begging someone to bring her the photo album that contained pictures of Ryan when he was young.

Wren had been enraged at the sheriff's callousness. She knew he had intended to arrest her. Only Annalise's law enforcement savvy had kept that from happening. Wren's hands had been swabbed for gunpowder residue. When it wasn't found, she'd been told she was free to go.

For now.

If her arm hadn't been broken, she'd have been at the rehab center before the sheriff. Instead, she'd headed to the farmhouse to get the photo album.

The farmhouse that seemed to be on fire.

She shouted for Annalise to stay back and raced to the side of the house, feet pounding the packed earth and soft grass. She'd planned to pull up the shrubs that were edging too close to the siding this week. The Realtor Abigail had hired had suggested it.

Now her only concern was keeping the old house from burning to the ground.

"Wren!" Radley yelled, grabbing her good arm and dragging her backward. "Go back to the car. I'll handle this."

"In what world would that ever happen?" she replied, her voice tauter and sharper than she'd intended.

"In my perfect world," he muttered, letting go of her arm and running around the back of the house with her.

He knew she wouldn't back down, and he wasn't going to waste time trying to convince her to. That was one of Radley's strengths. He knew how to take charge and how to concede leadership to someone else if necessary.

"In my perfect world, there wouldn't be smoke billowing out from the back of my foster mother's house," she replied, sprinting up the porch stairs.

The back door was cracked open, the threshold singed black.

She slammed her good hand against the door, and it flew open, banging into the wall behind it. If Abigail had been there, she'd have chastised Wren. She wasn't, and neither was Ryan. The closest thing to a kid brother she'd ever had, he'd been living with Abigail after divorcing his wife of five years. Darla had moved to Boston after the divorce was final, and Ryan hadn't been able to afford the house they'd bought together. The property had gone into foreclosure.

Wren knew that had been a blow to his ego.

He'd prided himself on doing better than his biological family had, of making his way in a world that wasn't always fair or equitable. He'd been almost too prideful about his accomplishments, something she'd never had the heart to tell him. He was Ryan—bighearted and bigheaded.

Now he was gone.

She crossed the threshold, barreling into the kitchen.

A room that had always been Abigail's favorite, it had once had fifties vintage charm that permeated all Wren's best memories. Now it was a disaster, water flooding the floor, smoke billowing up from curtains that were smoldering.

"You have a sprinkler system here?" Radley asked, stepping into the kitchen behind her, his gaze darting from one corner of the room to the other. She knew he wasn't looking for a sprinkler system. He was looking for danger.

"No," she responded, toeing an old green garden hose that was snaking through the kitchen and into the dining room. "Someone turned on the garden hose."

"To put out the fire?"

"I can't think of any other reason." She inhaled, the harsh scent of smoke stinging her nose. "I think I smell gasoline."

"I was thinking the same. Someone set the fire, and then tried to put it out?" Radley grabbed the hose and tugged it back into the room, turning the nozzle to shut off the water that had still been flowing out of it.

"That wouldn't make any sense."

"Does any of this?" he asked, following her as she moved cautiously into the dining room.

Unlike the kitchen, it had no deep char marks on the walls. She was so busy noting the condition of the room that she almost didn't see the man splayed out on the sopping area rug near the table. His face was turned away, his hair wet, his clothes soaked. Her heart jumped.

"Titus?" she murmured, rushing to his side, every thought of the hose, the water and the fire gone. Even now, even after so many years apart, she would have known him anywhere.

Seeing him like this—unconscious and vulnerable—tore at her heart.

She touched his neck, feeling for a pulse and praying she would find one. She'd already lost Ryan. She didn't want to lose Titus, too.

His eyes flew open. Not green or blue. A shade of teal that reminded her of the sky at dusk.

"Wren?" He snagged her hand.

"What happened?" she replied. "Are you okay?"

"I think so."

"Is this our perp?" Radley asked, his hand hovering near the holster that was nearly hidden by his suit jacket.

"This is Titus. A friend of mine," she responded.

"That doesn't mean he's not the perp," Radley pointed out reasonably.

"I'm not," Titus bit out, his eyes blazing. "Your perps are gone." He got to his feet, Wren's hand still in his.

She could have pulled away.

She probably should have.

Their friendship had ended years ago.

She hadn't seen or heard from him since the day she'd told him she'd seen his wife with another man. She had thought she was being true to their friendship, honoring the honest and caring relationship they had.

He hadn't taken it that way.

He'd called her jealous and petty, and had accused her of lying.

And she had stepped out of his life.

Just like that.

The hurt had felt like the worst kind of betrayal. That he hadn't known her well enough to have discovered the truth about who she was and what she was capable of had nearly broken her heart.

She'd survived by walking away and cutting herself off from him the same way she cut herself off from anyone who didn't respect her boundaries. She had learned plenty of hard lessons watching her mother, and she had vowed to never repeat the mistakes she'd witnessed. She wanted mutual kindness in her friendships, mutual care and respect and affection in all the relationships in her life.

Titus had once ticked all those boxes.

And, then, he hadn't.

They were strangers now, and she had no business holding on to him as if they were more. But he looked unsteady, and she told herself she was offering him support he obviously needed. The truth was more complicated. It was about friendship and loyalty and years when they had been each other's staunchest supporters. It was about time passing, about all the days and nights when she shouldn't have been missing him but had.

It was about that same heart-jolting feeling she had always gotten when she'd stared into his eyes. It was about the kind of love that didn't stop because of hurt feelings and broken trusts. Not romantic love. Real and deep and abiding friendship.

"Perps? As in more than one?" Radley asked, inhaling deeply. "I smell gasoline in here, too."

"Because two men were trying to burn the place down," Titus said. "I walked in on them before they could get the blaze going enough."

"Did you see them?" Wren asked, pulling her hand from his because she needed to—she was a professional, and he was the possible victim of a crime.

"Yes. One looked like a kid. Maybe late teens, early twenties. Skinny. The other was older. Heavier. I didn't get a good look at him. I was too busy dodging the baseball bat he was swinging at my head." He touched the back of his skull, pulling his hand away and looking at it as if he expected to see blood on his fingers.

"I take it you weren't successful?" Wren probed the area he'd just touched and found an egg-sized lump. No broken skin. No blood. That didn't mean it wasn't a serious injury.

He winced away. "How'd you guess?"

"That huge bump on your head clued me in," she replied. "Can you call an ambulance, Radley?"

"Sure."

"That's not necessary," Titus cut in.

"You could have a fractured skull. Or a concussion."

"I'm not seeing two of everything. I

don't feel sick. I'm not disoriented. I have a headache to beat all headaches, but I think I'll be just fine. What we need are the police."

"Based on the number of sirens I hear, I'd say they're on the way," Radley said.

Wren could hear the sirens, too, their warning muted by walls and glass. Once the police arrived, she might not have a chance to retrieve the photo album. The sheriff's department was small and had limited resources. It could be days before the house was processed and cleared.

She didn't want to wait days.

Not when Abigail was so upset.

"I'm running upstairs for something. Meet me out front." She tossed the word over her shoulder as she sprinted into the wide hallway that led to the front staircase. Functional rather than ornate, it had thick newel posts and dark wooden stair treads. None of it seemed to have been touched by the fire.

"Wren!" Radley called, rushing after her. "You know better. This is a crime scene."

"And my prints are already all over it," she replied, jogging up the stairs, her wrist throbbing dully with each movement.

"It's not about your prints. It's about contaminating evidence and disturbing the scene."

"From what I can see, the perps didn't go upstairs." She hit the landing at a near run. She couldn't bring Ryan back for Abigail, but she could at least do this.

"You may not be seeing everything."

"She's seeing enough. No gasoline trail up here. No burned carpet. No sign that they were trying to set it on fire." Titus cut in, following right on Radley's heels.

"That doesn't mean they weren't here," Radley reiterated.

"No, but I'm fairly certain the sheriff's office isn't going to have their investigation ruined by an FBI agent walking through the house she spent half her childhood in." Titus reached the landing and bounded up the stairs after Wren.

She could have joined the conversation, reminded them that she could handle herself and the situation. Under normal circumstances, she would have. These were not normal circumstances. Ryan's murder had pulled the rug out from under her, and she was still trying to regain her footing.

She walked into Abigail's room, trying not to notice the layer of dust on the once-immaculate dresser. She'd known that Abigail was getting older. She'd seen small changes in her at every visit. Less energy and verve. Less concern for keeping the house as spotless as it had once been. Overgrown lawn and weed-choked flower beds. Wren had told herself Abigail was busy with her church friends, her clubs and her volunteer work.

She had worried that it wasn't true.

But she hadn't visited more. She hadn't extended her stays. She hadn't asked Abigail flat out if she was able to handle the farm on her own.

She should have.

Just like she should have kept her mouth shut about Titus's wife. It was too late now. She couldn't change the past, but she could make certain that Abigail's future was secure, and that she had everything she wanted and needed.

She opened the closet, expecting to have to search the shelves for the album Abigail wanted. To her surprise, it was sitting on the floor near Abigail's shoes, Ryan's school pictures filling little oval slots on the cover. She tucked it under her arm and turned to leave the room, nearly bumping into Titus.

Surprised, she stumbled back.

"Careful," he said, grabbing her arm to steady her.

"I'm fine." She shrugged away, determined to keep distance between them. She didn't want to fall back into the trap of caring. She didn't want to be hurt like she'd been before.

"Is that the album?" Radley asked.

"Yes."

"Album?" Titus eyed the thick book.

"Abigail heard about Ryan's death. She wanted me to bring this to her."

"Heard about it?"

"The sheriff broke the news to her."

"He couldn't have waited for you to do it?"

"Considering I'm his prime suspect, I'd say he probably wanted to ask questions about our relationship."

"You and Ryan got along well most of the time."

"We did, but he was encouraging Abigail to sell the farm. I wasn't as excited about it."

"That doesn't make you a killer," Radley intoned.

"No, but it could be motive." It's certainly a motive she'd be considering if she were the investigating officer.

The first responders had arrived, firefighters banging on the front door asking if anyone was inside. She ran to open it, bracing herself for the chaos she knew was coming.

Wren hadn't been exaggerating when she had said that she was the prime suspect in Ryan's murder. Once the sheriff had arrived, he'd questioned Titus, put out a BOLO for the perps and then begun questioning Wren. He didn't come out and accuse her of setting fire to the house to cover up evidence, but he hinted that it might be a possibility. Titus listened silently, leaning against the mailbox at the end of the driveway as Sheriff Camden Wilson volleyed one question after another in Wren's direction.

"Sheriff, my client has already answered these questions," the FBI lawyer Wren had introduced Titus to cut in. She'd exited a black SUV as soon as the sheriff had arrived, her blond hair and fair skin contrasting sharply with her black suit. He should remember her name, but his mind was still foggy from the hit he'd taken.

"Not to my satisfaction."

"You have three witnesses who can all testify that Agent Santino was not here at the time the fire began—"

"She could have hired someone."

"Before or after you questioned her? During or after her wrist was set? At what point do you think she had access to a phone and the ability to make a call without being noticed." She crossed lean arms over her waist and eyed the sheriff dispassionately. She looked to be in her late thirties or early forties, fine lines near the corners of her eyes and a few strands of white mixed with her dark blond hair. She wore minimal makeup, a conservative suit and a half smile that Titus knew was getting under the sheriff's skin.

"What I'm saying is that she could easily have set all this up ahead of time." He glanced toward the house, frowning as he spotted the fire marshal moving toward them. "We can take up the conversation later. I need to speak with the fire marshal."

"I'm assuming my client is free to go?" the lawyer said.

"For now. Are you planning to leave the scene, Titus?" he asked. They knew each other from church but didn't run in the same circles. On a first-name basis but not friends.

"Yes." He hadn't put any thought to it. He'd been too busy trying to figure out why the sheriff would think Wren had murdered her foster brother. Now he was certain he wasn't sticking around. Not if Wren was leaving.

Whatever was going on, it wasn't good, and she seemed to be right at the center of it.

"Can you come to my office tomorrow to make a statement?" the sheriff asked.

"Tomorrow is Sunday," he pointed out.

"Crime has no favorite day of the week, and my office stays open 24/7 all year long. If you'd prefer to wait until Monday, that's fine, but we can move the case along more quickly if we have all the information we need."

"I'll be there after church. Maybe noon?"

"Whatever time suits you. You're not a suspect. You're free to come and go as you please." He shot a dark look in Wren's directions but didn't lob accusations at her.

He knew the limit of the law.

He seemed willing to bide his time.

He also seemed convinced she was responsible for the two crimes he was investigating.

"You're heading to the rehab facility?" Titus asked, stepping into place beside Wren as she walked to a black SUV.

"Yes."

"Mind if I come along?"

"Why?"

"Because I should have visited Abigail a long time ago and didn't."

"Now is probably not the time." She opened the back door of the SUV and slid in. She would have closed it, but he grabbed the top of the window and held it open.

"I'm going. If I have to drive myself, that's fine, but with the headache I've currently got, it's probably not the wisest choice."

She frowned, her forehead creased, her usually perfectly styled hair falling around her shoulder in wild waves. She had smudges of dirt on her cheek and shadows under her eyes, and she looked...

Tired?

Worried?

Sad?

Maybe all those things. Years ago he could easily have read the expression on her face and in her eyes.

Now he wasn't sure what she was feeling or thinking.

"We could give you a ride to the hospital," she suggested. "Or back home."

"I'd really like to visit Abigail and offer

my condolences. I know how much Ryan meant to her."

Mentioning Ryan seemed to loosen something inside Wren. She sighed, her shoulders bowing as she pulled her injured wrist closer to her chest. "All right. We'll give you a ride. When we return, I'll have Radley take you home."

"So, that's the kind of job a guy gets when he travels from Boston to help you? Chauffeur?" Radley asked as he got into the front passenger seat.

"There are worse gigs," the attorney said. "Go ahead and get in, Mr. Anderson."

"Titus," he corrected as he rounded the SUV and did as she asked.

"And you can call me Annalise." She started the engine and pulled away from the house.

Annalise.

Right.

He'd remember that.

Hopefully.

The throbbing ache in his head wasn't

doing much to motivate him. All he really wanted was to take a nap. Not a good choice with a head injury.

"You're not falling asleep, are you?" Wren's voice speared into his conscious, and he realized he'd closed his eyes and was drifting off.

"I was thinking about it," he admitted.

"Don't," she commanded, her gaze focused on the window and the world outside. She was doing her best to ignore him. He couldn't blame her, but he didn't like it.

"You're getting bossy in your old age, Wren."

That got her attention.

She whirled to face him, her dark eyes flashing. "Old? You're a year older."

"Ten months," he corrected, as if she didn't know or couldn't remember.

She did.

Wren had an uncanny memory and a keen intellect that had made her stand out in middle and high school. Based on how far she'd come since her years at the university, he'd say she hadn't changed.

"I know." She sighed. "You need to stay awake for a while. Closed head wounds can be just as dangerous as open ones."

"I know."

"So…" She glanced toward the front of the vehicle and lowered her voice. "Why are you here instead of at the hospital?"

"I already told you, I want to see Abigail."

"That's not the only reason." It was a statement rather than a comment.

"You're right. It's not," he said with a shrug. "I don't like what's gone down. You seem to be at the center of it, and that worries me."

"I see. You want to play knight in shining armor and rush to my rescue?"

"I want to be the friend I should have been nine years ago," he replied.

Her eyes widened just enough to show that he'd hit a nerve.

"The past is the past, Titus. How about we not bring it up?"

"I owe you an apology."

"And this is your way of giving it? Riding to the rehab facility with me?"

"Offering you support."

"I have support." She waved her hand at her coworkers.

"Now you have more," he replied.

She frowned. "This isn't the time or the place to discuss what I think about that."

"Good."

"But we *will* discuss it," she continued, turning away again.

He studied her profile, tracking the angle of her chin and the smooth plane of her cheeks. She was an older, more stunning version of the teen he'd spent so much time with. More polished. More streamlined. Even with her hair falling in tangles and her clothes ripped and stained, she looked sophisticated and professional. Everything she'd once told him she wanted to be.

I'll never be like her.

How many times had she said that?

When they were teens and young adults, it had been a constant theme in her life. She worked hard to assure herself that she would never be like her mother.

"If there is a choice between you staring at me and you sleeping," she murmured, "I'd prefer you to sleep."

"Even with a head injury?" he asked, curious to hear her response.

She glanced his way, the frown still in place. "No," she replied. "So how about we discuss what isn't going to happen."

"Between us?"

"There is no us. There is a volatile situation that I don't want you involved in," she replied.

"Unfortunately, you're not going to get what you want, because I'm already involved."

"No—"

"This got personal the second someone trespassed on my property and began shooting. I'm not going home and forgetting that happened."

And he wasn't going to forget that they had once been good friends who would never have turned their backs on the other's troubles.

If Wren thought that he was going to turn his back on her now, she was wrong. Despite the past, despite the hurt that was between them, he still cared, and he was still willing to do whatever it took to make certain she stayed safe. If that meant accompanying her wherever she went until the perpetrators were behind bars, then that was exactly what he planned to do.

FOUR

Abigail had faded in the hours since Wren had last seen her. She lay in bed, her tight silver curls flat against her head, her glasses perched on the edge of her nose as she flipped through the photo album Wren had brought to her.

"He was such an imp," she said, her eyes filling with tears. She touched the photo, her finger tracing across Ryan's smiling face. "Always smiling. Always happy."

"Always causing trouble," Wren added, hoping it would make Abigail smile.

It did, but even that couldn't hide the grief in Abigail's eyes. "That, too. Unlike you, he never did seem to settle into the routine of home and family."

"He did. It just took him a little longer."

"He didn't," Abigail corrected, smiling down at a photo of Wren and Ryan sitting in front of a Christmas tree. "If he had, he wouldn't be divorced."

"People do get divorced, Abby. Even people who want to settle into the family-and-home routine." She glanced at Titus. He'd taken a seat across the room, his back to the wall, his gaze on the window that looked out over the parking lot.

Radley was outside the room, guarding the door.

As if someone might barrel in and pull a gun.

After what had happened the past few hours, anything seemed possible. Anything *was* possible. Of course, she'd known that before she'd heard the gunshot that had killed Ryan.

"I know people get divorced. I am not a child in need of reminding," Abby huffed, her finger still on the photo. "But the reasons Ryan's marriage failed were ninety-nine percent his doing. He wanted to be out fishing and hunting and playing with the boys. Darla wanted to build a family. She wanted to save money for their future. He wanted to spend it."

"She told you that?" Wren and Darla had never been close. She'd tried to like the woman Ryan had brought into their makeshift family but Darla's slow-energy approach to her life goals had been frustrating. Seven years younger than Ryan, she'd been a flighty young adult when Wren had been introduced to her. Darla had talked about college dreams. She'd said she wanted to open a daycare center in town.

"No. Ryan told me that." Abigail's voice broke on his name. After she cleared her throat, she continued. "After she gave him the ultimatum."

"Ultimatum?"

"She wanted him to settle down. Stop going out all the time with the guys. Commit to having children and being a family. She wanted him to stop spending money and start saving it. Put something aside for their future. He was blowing all their earnings. He'd taken out a second mortgage on their house to finance that fishing excursion he went on with his buddies last fall. Did you know that?"

"No. I didn't." She'd loved Ryan, but they hadn't been close, either. They'd been complete opposites in every way. Except for their love for Abigail.

"He wouldn't have told you, because he knew you didn't approve of him."

"I approved."

"You approved of his job with the sheriff. You approved of the settled life he pretended to have. I did, too, so I'm not judging. I had no idea he was making such poor financial decisions while Darla worked two jobs and tried to put herself through college."

"She was in college?"

"As far as I know she still is. Getting a degree in early childhood education. She really settled down the last few years, but you wouldn't know that. You've been busy with your life." Abigail smiled to take the sting out of the words.

They still stung.

Because they were true.

"Ryan never mentioned it," she said by way of explanation, as if that somehow took the weight of her responsibility off her shoulders.

"Why would he? He was self-absorbed. We both know that. But he planned to make things right with Darla. He was going to save enough money to buy the house back from the bank. Now, I guess he won't have the opportunity."

"No. I guess he won't."

"I'll have to call Darla."

"Do you have her contact information?"

"Of course. We've grown close the last few years. She's turned into a lovely young woman. My address book is right here." Abigail set the photo album on the nightstand, opened the drawer and took out a small leather-bound book that she'd had in a drawer in the kitchen for as long as Wren had lived with her. She handed it to Wren. "It's in there. You can take that with you, but you'd better return it."

"That's okay. I'll just put the number in my…" She planned to say *phone* but remembered she didn't have one. The police had collected it as evidence and still hadn't returned it to her. "I'll call her later." She tucked the book into the back pocket of her jeans.

"You know," Abby said quietly, "this doesn't seem real, and it doesn't seem right. I'm an old lady."

"You're not old."

"I'm old," she reiterated. "I've lived a long, full life. I'm ready to meet my Lord. Ryan had a lifetime ahead of him. He should have had decades to build the family he said he wanted with Darla." A tear slipped down her cheek, and Wren wiped it away.

"I'm so sorry, Abby. I know how much you loved him."

"As much as I love you. And you're sitting there with your arm in a sling. What's going on, Wren? What's this about? It can't just be a random crime. Not in a place like Hidden Cove."

"I don't know, but I plan to find out," she promised.

"You'd better, because the way Sheriff Wilson was talking, I'd say you're high on the list of suspects."

"That's the way it always is, Abby. They look at romantic relationships and family first. Then they expand their circle of suspicion. They'll turn their attention away from me eventually." At least, they should. She knew how investigations worked. She understood that the sheriff and his team had to carefully review the evidence they collected. Beyond that, she wasn't sure there would be much effort to find another suspect. During her conversations with him, Wren had gotten the impression that the sheriff was eager to pin the shooting on her.

"You'd know that better than me, hon," Abigail said, closing the photo album and setting it on the nightstand. "Thank you for bringing that to me. I know it's silly, but I wanted to see pictures of Ryan at happier times."

"You know I'd do anything for you," Wren responded.

"*Anything* is a big word." Abigail raised a brow, her dark green eyes gleaming with calculation.

"Anything that won't get either of us into trouble," Wren added hurriedly.

"I want out of here. I'm sick and tired of being treated like an invalid. I want to go home. I think you can make that happen."

"You're being released at the end of the next week, and you're moving into the retirement home," Wren reminded her. "That's why I'm here, remember? To pack things up and help you move."

"My hip might be broken, but my brain is still working fine." Abigail sounded more like herself, the words a little sharp.

"I know when I'm supposed to be re-leased. I know I'm supposed to move into the retirement home. But, I want to go home first. I don't see why that should be a problem."

"Abby…" She hesitated, not wanting to explain what had happened at the farm-house. She hadn't heard from the sheriff or the fire marshal and had no idea how extensive the damage was. Keeping quiet until she had more information seemed prudent. It also seemed healthier for Abi-gail. She'd broken her hip and lost a foster son that morning. Hearing that the farm-house had nearly burned to the ground might be more than she could handle.

"We have to plan Ryan's funeral." Ab-by's voice broke, all the sharpness seeping out of it. She pushed the sheets and blan-kets aside. "Get me that walker, Titus," she demanded, gesturing to the hot-pink rolling walker Wren had purchased.

"Sure thing," he responded, his voice a warm, rich baritone. Wren had forgotten how soothing it could be. How calm he had always been. When they were teens, she had moved at lightning speed, rushing from activity to activity, checking things off her to-do list. He'd moved at a slower pace, reasoning things out and then springing into action when he had the full plan in place. He'd been the calm to her storm, and she'd loved that about him.

Loved?

Liked.

She had liked the way he'd approached life. She had liked the way he had approached people—with respect and compassion and a firm understanding of what he expected and what was expected of him. She had liked that he had cared about her in a way no one else ever had. At that age, she had doubted Abigail's commitment. She had doubted the support and encouragement of her teachers and counselors. She had never doubted Titus.

"Abby, you can't just get up and leave." Wren wrapped her good hand around Abigail's elbow as she got to her feet. She still had a limp from the fall and the surgery that had followed, but she was steady as she moved to the wardrobe to grab clothes.

"I am not leaving. I'm getting dressed and ready for the day. Sitting here mourning and crying and giving in to self-pity isn't going to accomplish anything. Unless I miss my guess, everyone in Hidden Cove knows what happened to Ryan. I'll have visitors all day. I need to get ready for the onslaught. You can work your magic with the doctor and nurses, and I'll be ready to break out of this place tonight."

"I don't think that's going to happen," Wren began, but Titus had pushed the walker to Abby's side.

"Here you go, Abby," he said.

Abby smiled. "You always were the most helpful young man. Thank you, Titus."

"No thanks necessary."

"Thanks are always necessary. Good manners are good habits. Haven't I always told you that?"

"Yes. You have." He towered over Abby, his six-foot-two frame dwarfing her four-feet-eleven inches.

"And we would both agree that not visiting an old friend for years and years on end isn't good manners, wouldn't we?" she continued, her dark green eyes focused on him.

Good. That gave Wren time to decide whether or not to broach the subject of the fire-and water-damaged farmhouse.

"We would," Titus replied, reaching into the wardrobe and pulling out the caftan Abby had been trying to remove from the hanger.

"Humph," she said, taking it from him and laying it on the seat of the walker. "Then, what is your excuse for not visiting me? You've been back in Hidden Cove for years. You've made a good name for yourself in the restoration business. People are always talking about what great work you do, and yet you have never once been out to see me or asked if I needed help with the farmhouse."

"I apologize, Abby. Life—"

"Is not so busy that we can't take time for one another. The years pass quickly. One day, you'll be my age, and I'll be long gone and buried. Will you be happy with the time that you wasted *not* being there for people you care about?" she demanded.

Titus shot Wren a look of desperation. When they'd been younger, she had always taken the hint and distracted Abby. But that had been years ago. They'd been best of friends, each other's biggest supporter.

When she didn't step into the conversation, Titus ran a hand over his short-cropped curls and sighed. "No. I won't be happy with it."

"That's what I thought." Abby nodded. "Seeing as how you've agreed that you need to spend more time with me—"

"Abby, he never said that," Wren broke

in, unable to stay out of the conversation for a minute longer. She knew where this was heading, because she knew her foster mother.

"I implied it," Titus responded.

"No you didn't," she argued.

"Are you two going to bicker like children?" Abigail asked as she rolled the walker to the bathroom door. "Because I personally don't think we have time for it. The farmhouse needs repairing quickly. From what Daniel said—"

"Daniel?" Wren asked.

"He's rehabbing from rotator cuff surgery. He had a minor stroke after, and his doctors wanted him to have more intensive therapy. So, he's down the hall. He's a retired firefighter. Called me this morning because he heard about the fire at the farmhouse on his scanner. He called the fire marshal at my request. Apparently, the old house is waterlogged but not terribly damaged."

"You know? Why didn't you say something?" Wren asked, hurrying to open the bathroom door.

"The question is, why didn't you? Do you think I can't handle more heartache? I haven't lived to be eighty-two without seeing more than my fair share of it. We'll get through this, but I want the best person available to do the restoration. Titus is it. That being the case, the two of you had better learn to get along."

"We know how to get along," Wren responded.

"Good. When can you start work on the house, Titus?"

"Immediately," he said.

Of course. He had always been the kind of person who could be depended on. One who jumped in to help when it was needed. Apparently, that hadn't changed in the years they'd been apart.

"Wonderful! We'll work around your schedule, of course. I do know how busy you are. I've heard so many good things from so many of my friends, I have every expectation that the work you do will be stellar. I'll pay half your fee up front. Half when you finish."

"No charge, Abby."

"Of course, you'll be paid," Wren said.

"We can discuss that later. I need to shower and dress. I know the pastor and some of the ladies from my Bible study will want to come visit and pray with me. I'll admit I'm not in the mood for visitors." Abigail's face fell, all the fine lines and wrinkles from decades of life suddenly showing. "But friendship buoys us up when we feel like we're drowning." She blinked back tears. "Are you going back to the house, Wren?"

"I thought you might want me to stay with you for a while."

"We'll plan the funeral later. For now, let's both have our time to grieve. Go back to the house. Make certain it's not worse than the fire marshal says. Call me with the details." It was a command rather than a request.

Before Wren could reply, Abigail had stepped into the bathroom and closed the door.

"I guess we have our marching orders." Titus broke the sudden silence, his voice invoking a hundred pleasant memories of nights spent exploring the shore and the forests, of days eating ice cream on the dock or walking through town together.

"You don't have to do this, Titus. You're under no obligation to my family."

"I can remember a time when you included me in that," he said.

She met his eyes, planning to tell him that those days were long past, that they weren't even friends any longer; something in his gaze kept her silent. A hint of sadness or longing. A silent plea for understanding and forgiveness.

She had already given the latter, but she had no intention of offering the first.

"I need to get back to the house," she said, turning on her heels and striding from the room. Radley was already on the move as she exited, heading down the hallway toward the elevators as if he'd heard every word that had been spoken. He probably had.

"I spoke to Annalise," he said as he pushed the elevator button. "She's been in touch with the fire marshal and the sheriff. We're cleared to go back in the house."

"Is she in the SUV?"

"Yes. Parked in front of the building." The doors slipped open and he stepped in.

She followed, ignoring Titus as he slammed his hand against the closing door and joined them.

The ride back to the farm was mostly silent. Wren asked a few questions of her coworkers, ignoring Titus. That was fine. He understood her anger. He knew it stemmed from hurt. If she'd had her way, she would have kept away from him for the rest of her life.

That was the way Wren was. Loyal to a fault until her loyalty was proved unfounded. Then she walked away and never looked back. He had seen her do that twice. Once during high school when she had dated the captain of the debate team. Brian Milton had been about as much of a geek as anyone could be, but he had been smart and driven. He'd had goals and dreams. Wren had been impressed by that, and she had agreed to a first date and then a second. Before Titus had time to realize what was happening, she and Brian were an item, holding hands in the hallway at school, going out together, sitting with one another at church. He had felt like a third wheel, which was an odd feeling since he'd had a girlfriend and didn't need to cling to Wren for companionship.

Six months into the relationship, Brian had made the mistake of flirting with one of Wren's friends. She'd cut him off like they'd never been together—a quick and well-deserved boot to the curb that had left Brian begging for a second chance.

Wren hadn't given it.

She'd done the same to her college boy-
friend—another nerdy guy she'd met in a
physics class. He'd raised his voice and his
hand to her one time. She'd punched him
hard enough to break his nose, called the
police and moved on with her life.

Titus had always cheered her on. He had
always admired the strength it took to love
and walk away the minute it became clear
that Wren's boyfriends didn't really love
her. He knew her backstory. He knew that
her mother had jumped from one bad relationship to another, always looking for
the next man to take care of her.

Wren had vowed to never be like that.
She had promised herself that she would
only be in relationships that were mutu-
ally beneficial and that she would never
stay with someone who hurt her.

She had made good on her promise to
herself.

Titus respected that, but he didn't much
like being on the receiving end of her
commitment to that vow. He hadn't meant

to hurt her, and he would have done anything to mend what had he had broken between them. But, she had cut him off without a word, walking out of his life and never looking back.

He watched as she climbed out of the SUV and headed around the back of the house. She didn't wait for Radley or Annalise, and she didn't seem to be concerned about her welfare.

Titus was concerned.

Ryan's murder had been a precursor to the fire at the farmhouse. Until they understood what had prompted the crimes, they had no way of knowing how to stop the perps from acting again.

"Do you need a ride back to your place?" Annalise asked, her light blue eyes devoid of emotion. She had a good poker face, one that probably served her well in court.

"I have a ride." He pointed to his vehicle.

"And you think you should be driving with a head injury?"

"If I didn't think I would be okay, I wouldn't do it."

"All right." Annalise shrugged. "It's your call. Do me a favor. If the sheriff interviews you about what happened this morning, let me know." She handed him a business card, and he tucked it into his wallet.

"I'm going to be giving him my statement tomorrow."

"I'm not talking about the fire. We'll have no problem clearing Wren of those charges. She was with me and Radley at the time it was set. I'm more worried about what happened prior to that."

"Ryan's murder? I wasn't there. I have no idea what went down."

"You saw her immediately afterward. She went to your place for help."

"She did."

"The sheriff might try to get you to reevaluate what happened."

"Reevaluate or reinvent?"

She shrugged again. "It'll be the same

result either way. He wants to arrest her for murder. I'm sure he legitimately thinks she's guilty. After all, she was at the scene. She is a family member, and that puts her at the top of the suspect list. My concern is that he'll try to influence eyewitness testimony to get the results he wants."

"You don't have to worry. I'm not easily swayed from what I know is right."

"You'd be surprised at how many people believe that about themselves and are surprised to find out they're wrong. I'm heading inside. Give me a call." She strode to the back of the house.

Wren and her coworkers seemed to think he was heading home, but he'd been hired to do a job. The sooner he began, the better. If that put him in close proximity to Wren, he wasn't going to complain. She might think that being arrested was the only thing she had to fear. He'd been back in Hidden Cove for enough years to remember just how closely the town guarded its secrets and protected its residents. He and Wren—even after all these years—were still outsiders. It would be easier for the community to believe she was guilty than to look for homegrown suspects. The blinders tied on by community loyalty could be dangerous. Until the perpetrator was caught, a murderer would remain free. And, as long as that was true, Titus wasn't going to trust that Wren was safe.

He walked to the back porch, jogged up the stairs and opened the back door. Wren, Annalise and Radley were standing in the kitchen. All three looked surprised to see him.

"I thought you left," Wren said, her voice sharp and tight. She didn't want him there. He knew that. Still, he couldn't convince himself to back away from the situation and let her and her team do what needed to be done.

"If Abby is coming home this week, I need to get started on the reno. I'm going to look around. Take some measurements and figure out what needs to be done."

He didn't ask permission.

He'd already been hired by the home-owner.

Wren frowned. "I'd prefer you wait until tomorrow."

"Why?"

"We're working," she responded.

"I'll be quiet." He walked into the dining room. She didn't follow. Years ago, they'd been nearly attached at the hip. Where one went, the other followed. He shouldn't miss those days; he didn't miss them.

But maybe he missed her.

He frowned, walking to the front door and opening it. He kept tools in his truck. He didn't need much. A notebook. Pen. Measuring tape. The floorboards in the dining room could be sanded down and refinished. The linoleum in the kitchen would need to be replaced. Once Wren and her team finished working, he'd check under the melted and scorched flooring. It was possible there was old tile or hardwood beneath it. That was one of the things he loved about restoration work. There were often cool things hidden behind ugliness. Police work had been the opposite. Smiling faces often hid dark thoughts and ugly souls.

He walked onto the front porch. A few of the boards were loose, the paint peeling in several areas. The railing needed to be sanded and refinished. The entire structure needed to be weatherproofed and secured. He'd been here hundreds of times as a kid. Now he was seeing it through the eyes of an adult. One trained in restoring properties just like it.

Abigail hadn't asked him to do anything more than fix the fire-and water-damaged areas, but he didn't think she'd mind if he did a little work for free. If she planned to sell the place, it needed to pass inspection.

He touched the banister at the top of the porch stairs. He would visit the town historical society to find out what color the porch had been originally. Maybe he'd check into the siding color, as well.

He strode down the stairs and across the yard.

The day was eerily quiet, the sky edged with dark clouds. This time of year, winter storms were still a possibility. He hadn't had time to check the weather, and it looked like one was blowing in. He'd take the measurements, make his list and then head home to draw up a contract for the work. Abigail wouldn't like it, but she'd be getting a steep discount. When he had been a young teen, she had been the only adult who had stood consistently by him. His teachers had tried, but he had been a troubled kid with a troubled home life. His grades had always been excellent, but his attendance and attitude had left a lot to be desired. They'd done what they could in the classroom to encourage him, but it had been Abigail who had cooked him meals and made him feel like someone cared.

He hadn't forgotten that.

She'd been right when she'd chastised him for not visiting sooner. She had offered him what no other adult could or would. He owed her a lot for that.

He grabbed a clipboard and notebook from the truck, took his tape measure out of the toolbox he kept in the back and headed around the side of the house. To his right, green lawn stretched to golden fields. For as long as he had been in Hidden Cove, Abigail had maintained a working farm. She grew acres of corn that she donated to food banks and churches. She had a small apple orchard and a few other fruit trees. She had taught every kid who had walked through her door how to sow and how to reap. No one left the farm hungry for food or for knowledge. She had always made sure of that.

Now, though, the place looked neglected. The fields were overgrown and untended. A two-story garage stood near the edge of the yard, Ryan's beat-up Ford Mustang parked nearby. From what Titus had heard, Ryan had moved into the garage apartment after he and his wife divorced and his house had been foreclosed on.

It was a bad deal, but Ryan had never seemed upset about it. Every time Titus had seen him, he'd been his normal jovial self. Had there been more going on his life than he'd let on? Had he been hiding things from his family? Keeping secrets from the world?

The door to the second-floor apartment opened, the movement so unexpected that Titus's heart skipped a beat. A man darted out. He was broad shouldered and heavy, and his bald head gleamed in the muted sunlight.

"Hey! What are you doing up there?" Titus called, sprinting for the building.

The guy was already down the stairs and racing across the yard. He made it to the cornfield a few hundred yards ahead of Titus and ducked into the dried-out stalks, disappearing from view.

Titus kept running. There'd be an unmistakable trail through the cornfield—broken and smashed stalks. He was halfway there when the silence was shattered by gunfire.

He threw himself to the ground and crawled to the nearest tree, ducking behind the thick trunk as he pulled his gun from its holster and got ready to fire.

FIVE

Three gunshots fired in rapid succession.

Then silence.

Another gunshot, and then Radley shouted for her to stay inside while he went out to investigate.

Wren knew the most reasonable thing to do was exactly that. Stay inside and out of the way. Stay out of trouble and out of the sheriff's line of sight. Rushing into danger would only put his attention squarely on her again. She would have to answer questions, explain her reasoning, justify her response.

She ran out the back door, pausing on the porch to survey the yard. There was no sign of gunfire or trouble. The green lawn rustled as a soft breeze blew through. Dark clouds edged in on the horizon, blocking the sunlight and warning of a coming storm.

Radley shouted, the words muffled by distance.

She ran in the direction of the sound, rounding the side of the house and crossing the yard. The cornfields were there—golden yellow, the old stalks still standing. Leaving them wasn't like Abigail. She either tended the fields herself or paid someone to do so. Last year she had done neither. Age creeping up on her, time stealing her energy and motivation. It was a normal part of life.

At least, that is what Wren had told herself when she'd visited in September. Just a weekend stay to make certain Abigail didn't need anything. It had been as obvious as the nose on Wren's face that she did and that someone should step in and help out. Ryan had been living in the house and, later, in the garage apartment that had once been a source of extra income.

Wren had tried to talk to him, explain that the farm was falling behind its seasonal schedule, but he'd had financial problems and was working overtime.

So she'd left, telling herself that she'd handle the problem when she visited for Christmas. If it still existed.

It had, but Wren had been working a case, and all her thoughts and energy were being put to solving it. She had let the situation go. Again.

She wished she hadn't.

She wished she had insisted that Ryan help more. If she had, he might have cut back on his hours at work. He might have spent more time at the farm. Maybe he would still be alive. Maybe whatever had motivated someone to kill him wouldn't have happened.

It had to be work related.

An angry perp who had been released from prison and sought revenge. An unhappy loved one who thought their relative had been railroaded by the arresting officer. Revenge hits were always a possibility when a person worked in law enforcement. They weren't common, but they happened.

She dashed across the yard, her injured arm thumping against her chest, her wrist throbbing. She could feel the arm swelling. She knew she needed to do exactly what the doctor had told her—rest and elevate.

Still, she didn't know how to not rush in when things went south. She'd worked as a Boston beat cop, then made her way up the ranks and, finally, joined the FBI. She'd trained hard, she'd worked hard. She had sometimes spent upward of twenty hours in the office and on the street, pounding pavement to get the answers she needed to solve cases. Special Crimes was her passion. She couldn't rewrite history for the victims, but she could make sure they got justice.

She needed answers for Ryan. She needed to know who had taken his life and why. Not just to protect herself from prosecution, but to make certain justice was done. Accomplishing that was going to take more than waiting in the kitchen while someone else fought her battles.

She sprinted to the cornfield and found the place where someone had crashed through the old stalks. They'd been trampled down and broken. She could hear someone rustling through the field just ahead. It had to be Radley.

She followed, shoving through scratchy foliage, the loamy scent of decaying plants filling her nose. She wanted her gun. She wanted the heavy weight of it in her hand, but she had only her instincts and her ability to move quickly and quietly. Even in a place like this—with dead plants ready to crackle and break—she knew how to be silent.

She had honed the skill decades ago when she'd tiptoed through the mine field of her mother's abusive relationships. She had lost count of the number of boyfriends who had entered and exited their home. She couldn't remember any of them being kind. Her mother had always been too desperate for love to be picky about the men she allowed into their lives. When she was murdered by her second husband, Wren had been orphaned. She'd never known her father, had no aunts or uncles or grandparents to take her in. Her mother had been an only child who had cut ties with her family before Wren's birth. She hadn't had any good friends who would have been willing to finish raising her daughter. After her death, Wren had entered the foster system. She'd learned to silently open windows, drop from second-story bedrooms onto grass or into shrubs so that she could escape the confines of homes that had felt like prisons. It wasn't that her foster families had been horrible. It was more that she had never felt as if she belonged. Moving silently through houses filled with other family-less kids had been her way of staying out of the limelight. She had tried her best to be in-visible—to move through each new place-ment as quietly as possible.

She used the skill to her advantage, mov-ing quickly through last year's crop until she could see Radley. He barreled through with little concern for being heard.

"Radley," she said just loudly enough that she thought he would hear. She didn't want him swinging around with his gun in hand.

He glanced over his shoulder and frowned.

"You're supposed to be back at the house."

"I don't recall agreeing to that plan. Did you see anything?"

"Your friend. Heading into the cornfield."

"Titus? He's in the house."

"No. He's in this cornfield." Radley enunciated every word as if he wanted to make certain she heard and understood.

She had done both.

She didn't want to believe it was true. Titus had been a police officer years ago. She wasn't sure why he'd quit the force.

By the time she had heard about it, the two of them hadn't spoken in several years. He had the training to handle this kind of situation, but it had been a while since he'd used it. She didn't think now was a good time for him to see if he remembered his training.

"That's not what I wanted to hear," she muttered, moving past Radley so that she could lead. If there was danger up ahead, she'd rather face it ahead of one of her agents.

He put a hand on her shoulder. "I'm the one with the weapon."

"I won't get in the way if you need to use it."

"You know what I'm saying, Wren. Let me make certain things are clear."

She knew she should.

She knew how she'd want things done if the shoe was on the other foot and she was the one with the gun. But she'd already lost Ryan. The thought of losing someone

else she cared about was incomprehensi-
ble. "I'll be fine."

She stayed ahead, listening for the
sounds of someone fleeing through the
field. All she heard was the soft snap and
rustle of cornstalks as Radley moved
through them behind her.

"It's quiet," she murmured.

"I noticed."

"I don't like it."

"You think whoever fired those shots is
planning an ambush?"

"I don't know, but we should at least be
hearing Titus." Unless he was injured.

Or worse.

Her pulse jumped at the thought, her
stomach sinking. If something happened
to him because she had asked for his help,
she would never forgive herself.

"I've already called the local PD. I'm
sure the sheriff is going to be happy to
come out here again."

"As far as I can tell, the only time he's

happy is when he's trying to throw the book at an innocent person."

"As a member of Ryan's family and the last person to see him alive, you're high on the list of possible suspects."

"I know. I'm just pointing out that he seemed to get a lot of pleasure out of trying to arrest me." She had reached the far end of the field and stopped, peering out from between golden stalks. There was another field beyond the one they were standing in. Once upon a time it had been an alfalfa field, the crop used to graze and feed the horses Abigail kept. She'd stopped keeping horses after her last mare died. Soon after, she'd let the field go fallow.

Wren had been concerned that she was giving up on the farm, letting things go and not caring that it was happening. She'd kept quiet. She hadn't wanted Abigail to feel guilty for not keeping up on things. She certainly hadn't wanted to convince her to do anything she didn't want to. She had a right to whatever kind of retirement she wanted. She'd spent her life devoted to other people, and now she had every right to be devoted to herself and her dreams.

If her dreams were to live in an apartment at a retirement village, Wren wasn't going to tell her she shouldn't do it. As a matter of fact, she had returned to Hidden Cove to help Abigail prepare for the move.

It was still hard to see the once-bustling farm quiet.

She scanned the field and the area around it. A road bordered the property to the west, meandering through other properties and making its way back to a craggy, rock-strewn beach. She could just see the gray-black pavement snaking between Abigail's property and the neighboring farm. A man was racing toward it. At least, she assumed it was a man. All she could see was a dark figure rushing across the fallow field. A few hundred yards behind him, Titus was sprinting in the same direction. She wanted to yell for him to stop, but she didn't want to draw attention to her presence.

She darted out of the cornfield, racing across weed-choked ground. The dark figure reached the road. She didn't see a vehicle, but she heard an engine spring to life. Seconds later, a white sedan sped into view. It braked hard and the suspect jumped inside.

Titus reached the road just as the car accelerated away.

He stepped onto the road, watching as it disappeared.

She knew he was trying to get a look at the license plate. It wasn't safe, and he shouldn't be attempting it.

"Titus!" she yelled.

He glanced in her direction, and she could almost feel the intensity of his gaze.

"Back off!" she continued.

"I want the plate number," he responded, turning his attention to the car again. It braked, the squeal of tires on pavement a discordant note in the eerie quiet.

She was nearing the road, Radley pounding the dry earth and dead grass behind her. Dark clouds had edged out the sun, casting the day in deep shadows and gloom. Her feet hit the pavement as the car began to back up. Slowly at first and then more quickly, speeding backward the way it had come, heading straight toward Titus.

He was at a dead stop in the middle of the road, staring at the approaching vehicle. Reading the license plate number and trying to commit it to memory. She was certain of that.

But memorizing the license plate number wasn't going to do anyone any good if he was dead.

"Titus, move!" she yelled.

He didn't turn, didn't flinch, didn't acknowledge her in any way.

"This isn't the right time to play chicken!" she growled as she dove the last few feet, slamming into his side and pushing him out of the center of the road. He stumbled but didn't fall, his arm wrapping around her waist as the car zoomed past.

He would have pulled his gun if his arm hadn't been wrapped around Wren's waist, but he had a firm grip on her side, his fingers digging into solid abdominal muscles. She was lean and muscular, her strength honed from years training in the gym and out of it. Even after all this time apart, he knew that to be true. If she had wanted to, she could have freed herself. She could have used momentum and surprise to toss him off his feet and into the ditch at the side of the road. He had seen her teaching women's self-defense classes in college. He had watched her take down larger, stronger men. He had even helped her demonstrate technique. That had been nearly a decade ago, but based on her toned muscles, he would guess she had never stopped training. From what he knew about her past, he would say she had never stopped teaching self-defense classes. She believed in empowering women to fight their own battles.

He had always applauded that.

But she was injured, her arm wrapped in a soft cast. It slapped into his ribs as she whirled to face the car.

"Here he comes!" She grabbed his arm, yanking him off the road and into the drainage ditch beside it. The dry bed was filled with leaves and grass and debris.

"You should have stayed back at the house," he growled, jumping up as the car passed again. He darted out into the road, pulling his gun and shooting at the fleeing vehicle. The bullet hit the back window, shattering it.

"Stand down and get out of the way," Radley shouted.

He moved to the side, not bothering to rush. There was no hurry now. The car had disappeared around a curve in the road. They could chase it, but they'd never catch up on foot.

"Did you get the tag number?" Wren

asked as she climbed out of the ditch. There were smudges of dirt on her jeans. More on her shirt. Her hair fell to her shoulders, a tangled mass of waves that she had been securing in tight buns for as long as he had known her.

"Yes." He reeled it off, doubting it would help. The vehicle had probably been stolen and would be abandoned somewhere away from town. In an area like this—with dozens of side roads leading into mountains and wilderness, an abandoned vehicle would be difficult to locate.

"I'll call that in so the sheriff can put out a BOLO. Next time, you might want to stay out of it," Radley muttered.

"I don't believe in staying out of things when I think my help is needed," he said easily.

"Your idea of helping and mine aren't the same."

"What's that supposed to mean?" He met Radley's eyes and kept his tone even and light. No sense in going head-to-head with one of Wren's coworkers, but he wasn't going to back off, either.

"You were in my way. I could have taken out a tire and stopped the car cold, if you hadn't been standing on the road."

"You don't know that, Radley." Wren sighed. Her skin was pale, her eyes red rimmed and deeply shadowed.

"Sure, I do," Radley responded.

"How about we focus on fact rather than speculation?" She turned her attention to Titus. "What happened, Titus? How did you end up out here instead of in the house?"

"I was getting some tools from my truck. I saw someone walking out of the garage apartment, and I followed him."

"The garage apartment?" She frowned. "Ryan was living there. We had better check things out and make sure nothing is missing. Not that I know what he had," she said.

"I'll meet the police here. That'll give you a chance to look things over before the sheriff arrives," Radley said, and pulled out his cell phone.

"Thanks," Wren murmured, turning back toward the house and heading across the old alfalfa field.

Titus followed. He had no desire to speak with the sheriff. He remembered Camden from high school. Two years ahead of him, he'd been a loudmouth who had loved to tell everyone that his father was sheriff's deputy and best friends with the sheriff. He and Titus hadn't run in the same circles. And not just because they were in different grades. Titus had been a newcomer, and he had been a poor one. He and his mother had lived in the house she had inherited from her grandfather. Aside from the roof over their heads, they hadn't had much. Camden had been as close to royalty as anyone in small-town America could be.

Titus caught up to Wren, matching her pace as she moved quickly across the abandoned alfalfa field. Years ago, he had helped Abigail plant the fields. He had taken a lot of pleasure in watching the crops grow, and he had always been eager and willing to help with the harvest. Back then, the farm had been alive with animals and people and lush fields. Now it was a lonely, dead place.

"I know what you're thinking," Wren said as they entered the rows of dried-out cornstalks.

"What?"

"That this place is neglected. That Abby has let it go. Maybe that Ryan and I should have stepped in and helped before it got like this."

"Is that what you think? That you should have done more to help before it came to this?" He touched a dead cornstalk.

"Of course." She had always been honest and matter-of-fact. The kind of person who saw the world for what it was and loved it anyway.

"If Abigail had asked you to come and help, would you have?"

"I'm here because she asked. So, of course."

"Then you did everything you could. As far as Ryan goes, who knows?"

"What do you mean?" She shot a look in his direction, her dark lashes shadowing her eyes so that he couldn't read the expression in them.

"He was here. He saw it every day for… what?…a couple years?"

"He moved in after his house was foreclosed on. That was nearly three years ago."

"Right. He lived here. He knew what needed to be done to stop things from getting like this." He touched another dead cornstalk.

"He was busy trying to build up savings and get back on his feet, and we both know that he wasn't very good at doing work on the farm."

They had reached the edge of the field. The garage was to their right, red paint faded from too many bright summers and harsh winters. Ryan wasn't the only one to blame. Titus could have stepped in. He could have visited. He could have helped without being asked.

That was what family did.

And Abigail had always considered him that.

"You're right. Ryan wasn't great at working on the farm, but I always enjoyed it. I could have stepped in and helped," he admitted.

"Did she ask for your help?" Wren said.

"No."

"Then, you did what you could. We both know how stubborn Abigail can be when it comes to asking for and accepting help. So, how about we focus on other things?"

"Like?"

"You said you saw the perp coming out of the garage apartment?" Wren switched gears, her focus on the exterior stairs that led to the second-floor apartment. A small studio with a kitchenette, bed and living area, it had been rented out to hunters and fishermen when Titus was young. During the winter—when it was empty—Abigail offered it free of charge to anyone who needed a place to stay for a few nights.

He had stayed there on more than a few occasions, sick of his mother's drug-induced haze. Tired of cleaning up and cooking and being the parent in the home. He'd escaped to the garage apartment, Abigail's home-cooked meals and satisfying farmwork.

"Yes," he said.

"Let's go see what he was doing up there." She headed up to the apartment, taking the stairs two at a time.

He followed, stepping onto the landing behind her.

"The door is open," she said, eyeing the one-inch crack.

He wasn't sure if she was speaking to him or to herself.

"He was in a hurry." He responded anyway.

She nodded, using her foot to nudge the door open more.

She stepped inside, the soft inhalation of breath the only hint he had that something was wrong. He pressed in behind her, his shoulder brushing hers as he moved by and caught sight of the interior. The place had been ransacked. The couch was torn apart, the cushions slashed, the stuffing strewn across the floor. The mattress had been tossed off the bed, sheets left in a pile nearby. Pillows destroyed. Mattress gutted. Papers and books had been torn from shelves and drawers, and clothes littered the floor.

"He was definitely looking for something," he said, walking through the room and into the alcove that contained the kitchenette. The cupboards were empty, boxes and containers of food ripped apart, flour and cereal spread out on the floor and counters.

"What?" Wren asked.

This time he knew she was talking to herself. He could almost see her mind working as she glanced at the kitchenette and then walked into the only separate space.

"He went through the bathroom, too," she said.

He walked to the doorway and surveyed the small room.

Like the rest of the apartment, it had been torn apart, the linen closet emptied, everything tossed on the floor. "Was he carrying anything when he left?" she asked, turning to face him.

They were just feet apart, her eyes blazing the way they had when she was young and on a mission for justice. She had been the kid teachers either loved or found exasperating, her strong desire to learn and understand matched by her need for justice and truth. She had never been afraid to call a teacher out or correct misinformation. She had never let a point go. Not if she knew she was right.

He had loved that about her.

Loved? That was a strong word.

Liked. Admired. Applauded. Cheered.

"No," he said, bracing himself for the onslaught of questions he knew were coming. Unless she had changed a lot in the years since they'd spoken, she'd ask him to repeat every detail of what he'd seen until she was satisfied that she knew everything there was to know.

"You're sure?"

"Unless he was carrying it in a pocket or hiding it under his jacket."

"He was wearing a jacket?"

"Yes. Dark colored. Jeans. A light-colored shirt."

"So, the jacket was open?" She pulled a stepladder from the linen closet, her broken wrist cradled close to her stomach. He wanted to ask if she was in pain, suggest that she wait outside and let him look, tell her that she should take it easy.

But he had given up his right to try to influence her life when he had accused her of lying about Meghan. In retrospect, what he'd done made no sense. He had always known Wren's heart, and it had always been for what was right and good.

"Yes. It was open," he replied, taking the stepladder from her hand. "You're planning to go into the attic?"

"I want to see if he's been there."

"Wouldn't he have left this out?" He carried the stepladder to the living area and set it in the middle of the room. A small panel in the ceiling could be removed for access to the attic. Abigail kept exterior Christmas decorations there.

At least, she had.

"Probably, but I want to check. Whatever he was looking for, he was thorough in the search." She nudged a gutted pillow with her toe. "If he was in the attic, I want to see what he went through."

"Christmas decorations. Isn't that what Abby keeps there?" He climbed up and removed the panel, sliding it sideways and into the attic. Cold air seeped through the opening.

"A lot of Ryan's stuff was up there, too.

He had an entire house to store, remember? Come on down. I'll go up."

"You have a broken wrist," he pointed out, hoisting himself up. The attic stretched the length and width of the garage, the hand-hewn beams salvaged from a barn that had once stood on the property. Abby had told him that the first time he'd carried boxes of lights and outdoor decorations into the space. She'd been proud of the ingenuity her parents had shown in choosing to salvage old materials to create something new. She had planned to spend the rest of her life honoring the time and effort they had put into the beautiful property.

It didn't look beautiful now. One glance out the garage window, and he would be able to see the fallow fields and the overgrown orchards. The house needed to be painted, the porch whitewashed, the garden tended.

Had Abigail stopped caring or had age made it difficult for her to perform all the necessary chores. She had money. She could have hired someone, but she had always been a little proud and a little reticent when it came to admitting her weaknesses.

"See anything?" Wren's head and shoulders appeared in the opening.

"It's unremarkable. No open boxes. No shredded pages. Nothing that tells me he was here."

The attic was chock-full of stuff. Boxes stacked against boxes. A few bags. A trunk.

"It does look clean. He might not have known there was an attic." She tried to boost herself in, but she couldn't put weight on her bad wrist, and she slid down again.

"Here." He grabbed her under the arms, lifting her easily. His hands were on her upper ribs, his fingers nearly touching in the middle of her spine. He was looking into her eye, seeing the girl she had been and the woman she'd become.

"Titus," she said quietly, and he knew she felt what he did—the old connection that had carried them through adolescence and into adulthood.

The one broken by his accusations.

"I'm sorry," he said, knowing it wasn't the right time or place but worried there would never been another opportunity.

"For helping me into the attic? I was just about to thank you. The broken wrist is making life challenging," she said, her gaze skimming across the attic floor, dancing along the stacked boxes, focusing on anything but him.

He touched her cheek, his fingers grazing across her cool, smooth skin. She wore no makeup, and her skin was flawless. Aside from the faint scars on her neck and near her hairline, there was no hint of what she had survived. "You know what I'm talking about."

"The past is that, Titus. Past. I don't dwell in it, I don't revisit it, and I certainly don't want an apology for it."

"You deserve one. What I said and did—"

"Don't." She held up her hand as if that could stop his words.

It couldn't, but the look in her eyes did.

She was studying his face, focused—finally—on him. He was sure there was sorrow and regret in her gaze.

"What happened was for the best," she said finally, a blithe tone to her voice that aggravated him.

"How do you figure?"

"Your life was obviously heading in a very different direction than mine. We couldn't have remained friends forever."

"That's not what you said when we were kids," he replied, and she tensed.

"Right, because I was a kid. I believed in fairy tales and make-believe. I thought wanting something enough could make it happen, and I had no idea how life would change us."

"I hurt you, and I didn't mean to. I was—"

"In love," she cut in.

"An idiot," he responded.

Her lips quirked, and he knew she was fighting a smile. He touched the corner of her mouth, his pulse jumping in a way he hadn't expected and didn't want.

This was Wren. His old friend. His chum. His buddy.

She was also a stranger. A beautiful one.

"Tell you what," she said, turning away. "How about we stop talking about the past and start talking about the present. What do you notice about this place?"

"It's neat," he said, his focus jumping from one box to another and then dropping to the floor. Most of the attic was covered with dust. It was on the boxes, the trunk and the bags that had been tucked in a corner. But one section of the floor was clean, the area free of dust.

"Someone was up here." He crouched and moved to the cleared area. There was a box nearby, the tape seal cut.

"Not our perp," Wren murmured. "He wouldn't have been so neat."

"Ryan?" he guessed.

She shrugged. "Who else?"

"So, what's in the box?" He'd have opened it himself, but Ryan wasn't his foster brother. This wasn't his home. He had no right to do anything other than stand back and let Wren look.

"I don't know," she said, moving close, her arm and shoulder pressed against his, her hair brushing his cheek, and she leaned toward the box. Silky hair. Firm muscles. Narrow shoulders with scapulae that jutted from beneath her shirt.

He shouldn't be noticing any of that.

He shouldn't be thinking about it.

He shouldn't be fighting the urge to brush strands of hair from her cheek and let his fingers linger on her smooth skin.

"Let's see what's in here," she said, oblivious to his thoughts, instead totally focused on the task.

Which was exactly how she should be. How he should be. They were there to figure out who had killed Ryan and why. If there was a clue in the mess strewn across the apartment floor or in the box that had been neatly stored in the attic, they needed to find it.

So, he would focus.

He'd set his mind to the task at hand.

And, later, when this was over and the danger had passed and the person responsible for Ryan's death was in jail, he'd let himself think about the way he felt when he was close to Wren, and he'd spend some time figuring out exactly what it meant.

SIX

It wasn't a large box. Certainly not the size Abigail would have used to store Christmas decorations. Wren wasn't sure what she expected to see in it. Some clue, maybe, to what had happened to Ryan. Instead, there were stacks of gleaming brochures.

She took out one, frowning as she opened it. "Wonder why these are here."

"What are they?" Titus crouched beside her. She tried not to notice the warmth of his arm pressed against hers or the hint of soap and aftershave that seemed to drift around him. They had once been as close as two friends could be. She had known all his secrets, and he had known hers. That kind of bond was difficult to break.

When she'd stopped communicating with him, it felt like a piece of her soul had been taken away.

"Brochures for Sunrise Acres Retirement Village." She eased away from his warmth. It would be too easy to fall back into old habits, to allow herself to count on him, confide in him and trust him.

It would be just as easy for her to be hurt again.

Since she didn't believe in repeating her mistakes, she couldn't let that happen.

"I've heard good things about it." He reached for a brochure, turning it over to read the back.

"So have I. Abby is determined to move there. Most of her friends already have."

"Tennis court. Golf. Movie theater. Barber. Hair stylist. Spa. Who wouldn't want to live there?" he said, reading off the list of amenities.

"I'm aware of all the wonderful perks that go with living at Sunrise Acres," she said. She'd been hearing about them from the moment she had visited Abby at the hospital after she had broken her hip.

"You sound annoyed by that."

"Not annoyed. Just pragmatic. All those things come at a price."

"Yeah? I've never looked into that."

"Yes. Abby wants a two-bedroom condo with views of the cove. She's selling the farm to cover the cost. That's what most of the people who live there have done. Sold homes and property to afford a convenient lifestyle."

"There's nothing wrong with convenience," he pointed out, setting the brochure on the floor and lifting a stack bound with a rubber band from the box.

"I know," she agreed. She'd been telling herself that from the moment Abby had expressed a desire to sell the farm and move to the retirement village. The announcement had taken Wren by surprise. She had thought that Abby would spend the rest of her life on the farm her grandparents had bought and tended. She had known that there was no one to hand it down to. Abby was the last of the bloodline, and she had never married or had children.

Still, it hadn't occurred to Wren that Abby would sell the property she had poured her heart and soul into.

"Then why does it upset you? Because Abby is jumping on board?"

"I didn't say it upset me." She lifted a stack of brochures, more to have something to do than to take another look.

"You didn't have to. I know when you're upset."

"You *knew*. It's been a long time. I don't get upset as easily as I use to." That was the truth. She'd learned to control her sharp tongue and to choose her battles.

"When two people were as good of friends as we were—" he began.

"How about we stay focused on what we came up here for? I'd like to figure this out before the sheriff arrives and kicks us out." She cut him off. She didn't need to be reminded of how close they'd been. She didn't want to admit that it felt as if they could still be that.

"Right. We've got brochures for the new retirement home, and we want to know why." He lifted another stack and frowned. "These are different."

"Are they?" She leaned toward him without thinking, her arm pressing into his. He'd filled out in the past few years, biceps thick with muscle. She remembered him from their childhood—his lanky arms and legs and lean frame. He had been the only guy she'd known who'd been taller than her all through middle and high school.

"These are for a place in Florida." He pulled one out from the bundle and handed it to her.

If she hadn't been distracted by thoughts of Titus and their past, she would have already noticed it was different from the other brochures. Bright sunshine. Pristine beach. Beautiful condos and cottages that looked exactly like Sunrise Acres Retirement Village's, just in a different location. "What are these doing in there?"

"It looks like the same development company is building both retirement communities." He turned over a copy of each brochure and pointed to a name printed there.

"Garner Investment Initiative. Never heard of them." She took a copy of each and tucked them in her back pocket. More than likely, the contents of the box had nothing to do with Ryan's murder, the fire or the apartment being ransacked, but Wren didn't believe in leaving any stone unturned. She would have someone at the field office investigate Garner Investment. Just to make certain it was on the up-and-up.

"Me neither, but it's not surprising that an investment company wants to dip its toes in the retirement market. In places like Hidden Cove, where the community is aging and young people are moving away in droves, it's almost a certain moneymaking venture."

"Florida isn't a bad investment location, either."

"No, and if you're going to sell Florida property, this isn't a bad place to do it. Most people get tired of the cold weather and the long winters."

"Not you. Winter is your favorite season," she said without thinking.

She didn't want him to know how much she remembered about their years of friendship. She didn't want to admit— even to herself—how much she remembered about him.

She'd cut herself off from their friendship because she hadn't wanted to be hurt again, but her feelings had taken a long time to change.

"Yes. And fall is yours."

"The sheriff's department has probably arrived. I'd better go speak with them." She would have shimmied out of the attic, but he took her hand, his thumb running over her knuckles. There was tenderness in his touch and the kind of gentleness she wasn't used to. She was a law enforcement officer, a woman who had made her mark in a man's world. She knew how to take charge. She knew how to lead. She knew how to hide her pain and keep her emotions in check.

But she didn't know how to look away when Titus stared into her eyes.

"We can't avoid this forever," he said, his voice as gentle as his touch.

"Avoid what?"

"The elephant in the room. The thing that keeps making you run."

"I'm not running. I'm doing my job."

"Your job is to heal."

"My job is to find out who killed Ryan and to make certain that person pays. Ryan was as close to family as I have. I'm not going to sit back and wait for the local PD to figure this out."

"I'd feel the same, and I would be doing what you are. That doesn't change the fact that every time we're close, you scurry away."

"First, I don't scurry. Second, we haven't been close."

"Closer than you're comfortable with."

"I'm not going to deny that."

"Which begs the question. Why are you uncomfortable?"

"We were friends. Now we're not. That's all either of us needs to know. Now, if you don't mind, I really do need to go speak to the sheriff." She tugged away, slid out of the attic on her belly, her bad wrist and hand useless. He positioned his hands under her arms, supporting her as she descended.

It felt like old times.

Good and comfortable and right.

It wasn't any of those things. It was old habits that were rearing their ugly heads. It was hurt about to happen again. It was a second chance at losing a piece of her soul.

"Thank you," she said as her feet found the stepladder. She climbed down easily and didn't wait for Titus. She needed fresh air to clear her head and to rid her of the butterflies that were dancing in her stomach.

Because of Titus.

Because she had stared into his eyes and allowed him to hold her hand. Because he had helped her down and hadn't argued with her need to seek justice for Ryan.

He had been what he was to her all those years ago—a good friend, ready to help in whatever way was necessary.

That was a tempting thought.

To believe he could be depended upon. To allow herself to trust him. To give herself over to what had once been.

She couldn't afford to do any of those things. There was too much riding on her ability to stay focused. Ryan was dead. He'd been murdered. She planned to find his killer. And she wasn't going to let anything or anyone distract her from that goal.

Wren was stepping outside as Titus climbed off the stepladder. He followed, knowing that she wouldn't glance in his direction. She was running away again, and that was fine. He wasn't going to chase her down or try to get her to admit to feelings she didn't want to acknowledge. He knew they were there. He could see them each time their eyes met. He could feel them every time their hands touched.

Their friendship had been dormant.

If they allowed it, it would spring back to life.

He stepped onto the exterior landing.

Wren had already reached the ground and was jogging around the side of the house. The day was silent. No sirens breaking the stillness. No voices calling from the front of the house.

He could see strobe lights flashing on the ground at the side of the house. The sheriff or one of his deputies had arrived. Like Wren, Titus was interested in speaking to whoever it was.

There had to be some leads that pointed

to the real murderer. He was certain the trail wasn't leading directly to Wren, so who was it leading toward?

That was a question local law enforcement needed to answer.

Titus knew it would be best if he kept his nose out of it. But, like Wren, he wanted justice for Ryan. If that meant digging through boxes in attics, so be it. If it meant going head-to-head with the sheriff to get answers, he could do that, too.

What he couldn't do was go home and pretend none of this had happened. He couldn't walk to his car, drive away and go back to the life he had carved for himself.

No matter how much Wren might want him to.

He walked down the stairs and around the side of the only house that had ever really felt like home. He had asked Wren if she was upset that Abby was selling it. She had sidestepped the question, but he thought he knew the answer. She wanted what was best for Abby. She always had, but she didn't want the place sold. Her only good childhood memories had been made within the walls of the two-story farmhouse. It would be hard to say goodbye to a place that had offered her security, safety and peace.

It was also hard to see the woman they had both thought of as unstoppable and indestructible getting to a point where she could no longer care for the property she loved. Abby's broken hip had forced her into a decision that had been coming for a long time. All he had to do was look at the fallow and untended fields, the peeling paint and the weed-choked flower beds to know that.

Three cars belonging to the sheriff's deputies were parked at the front of the house, the officers who had driven them standing in the front yard. Wren was speaking to them, her hair gleaming in the gloomy light, her face colorless. Radley hadn't returned, but Annalise stood on the porch, arms crossed, blond hair pulled into a neat ponytail. She was tiny and cute, her heart-shaped face and large eyes belying her tough interior. He imagined she was cutthroat and aggressive in the courtroom, and that she took unsuspecting prosecuting attorneys by surprise.

She met his gaze, nodded and went back to staring at the sheriff's deputies. Wren had people in her corner. This wasn't like when they were kids—the two of them pitted against the world. He could leave and not worry that she would have to face her troubles alone. He could grab what he needed from the truck and return to the work he had been hired to do.

Even better, he could get in his truck, drive to the sheriff's office, give his statement and go home. He could plan the rehab of the farmhouse from there and leave Wren alone. It was what she seemed to want, but he couldn't make himself do it. There was too much between them still— all the memories of their teen years still taking up space in his head and his heart.

He had tried to forget her. He had often told himself that the bond they'd once shared hadn't been nearly as strong as he had recalled, but each time he looked into her eyes, he proved himself wrong.

The bond was still there.

If they allowed it, they could be pulled in again. They could rediscover their friendship, rebuild their relationship and be even closer than they had been when they were younger. Wren had established herself in her career. She had become everything she had ever said she wanted to be.

She hadn't married, though.

He would have heard about that through the grapevine.

Then again, he didn't recall her ever talking about a husband and kids and a white picket fence. He had dreamed of having a family and home. She had wanted a career and a home life devoid of the emotional chaos she had experienced as a child.

He walked to her side, felt her tense as

he took a position a foot away. Not close enough to touch. Close enough to offer support if she needed it.

"We'll go inside the apartment and dust for prints," one of the deputies said. Titus had done some restoration work for him— gutting the 1970s kitchen in his Cape Cod and returning it to its original 1920s charm. Levi Goodwin had been very clear on what he wanted. Everything as original as it could be. He'd even purchased a refinished 1920s stove. All for his wife, who had been in the hospital waiting for a stem cell transplant to treat bone cancer.

"Levi, how are you?" he asked, offering his hand.

"Great. My wife still loves everything about the kitchen. You do outstanding work. You going to do something here?" He gestured to the farmhouse.

"I'm cleaning up from the fire."

"Didn't realize you did that kind of work."

"I restore houses. I know people who do water and fire cleanup," he said.

Levi nodded. "Good. This place is a part of Hidden Cove history. We wouldn't want anything to happen to it. Wren said you saw the person who ransacked the apartment?"

"I caught a glimpse of him leaving the house."

"You got a look at his face?"

"Just height, body type and clothes."

"And you're the one who got the tag number?"

"That's correct."

"No mistake?"

"I'm sure of it."

"We ran the tag. It's registered to a young woman who reported it stolen last night. She finished her shift at work and discovered that her car was missing."

"That isn't surprising," Wren interjected, her focus sharp. She was like a dog with a bone when she began working on something. No matter how exhausting it might be, no matter how tired she got, she never stopped.

"No, it's not," Levi agreed. He smiled, but it was a quick, tight curve of lips. Nothing like the broad smiles and gregarious chatter he had offered while Titus worked on his kitchen.

"I'm not here to step on toes, Deputy," Wren began.

"Ryan spoke highly of you," Levi said, cutting her off. "He said you were a great law enforcement officer with a stellar reputation. So, it might be best for you to step back and let us do our job."

"I have no intention of interfering with your investigation. I'm just giving you information that may be helpful to it."

Levi nodded, his expression grim. "We're on the same team, Wren. It might not seem that way, but we are. We are just as eager to find out who killed Ryan as you are. He was a coworker and a friend, and we plan to get justice for him."

"I'm glad to hear that," Wren responded. "But justice isn't going to be served if your focus remains on me."

"We aren't only focusing on you," another officer said. Older by at least a decade, with bleached hair and wide blue eyes, Hannah Simmons had been a fixture in the Hidden Cove Sheriff's Department for as long as Titus had been in town.

No-nonsense and by the book, she was known to be both fair and tough. She accepted no excuses, but she often gave second chances.

"That's good to hear, Deputy Simmons," Wren replied. "But, at the moment, I seem to be the only suspect."

"You're not a suspect in my eyes," Hannah said.

"Everyone is a suspect until proven innocent," the third deputy said.

The youngest of the three, he looked fresh out of high school, a little acne on his chin, his hair slicked back from a high forehead.

"You've got that backward, kid," Hannah said with a sigh. "Innocent until proven guilty, and we currently have no proof that Agent Santino was involved in the murder. I, for one, find it hard to believe that she'd try to burn down Abby's home. And why would she need to ransack the apartment over a garage she has full access to?"

The young man blushed, his entire face going red. "Family members and significant others are always at the top of our suspect list," he managed to stutter.

"That's what the book says, kid, but we need to take a practical approach to police work," she replied easily.

She turned her attention to Titus. "How clear was your view of the perp?"

"He was bald. Heavy build. Muscular. As I already mentioned, I didn't get a good look at his face."

"According to the 911 caller, gunfire was exchanged." She took a notebook from her pocket and wrote something on one of the pages.

"Not exchanged. He fired at me. Several shots. I didn't fire my weapon until he tried to run me down with his vehicle."

"If you had shot him, it would have been self-defense." She jotted a few notes and then met his eyes. Titus had had a few run-ins with her during his teenage years. Usually because he was loitering at the local diner after it closed, hoping the owner would take pity on him and hand him leftovers to take home.

He'd been that kid.

The one that everyone knew and most people either feared or pitied. A brown-skinned newcomer in a town that had almost no diversity, he had been an oddity that had made some people nervous. He had often found himself facing the sheriff or a deputy, promising to go straight home after their talk.

"I couldn't see him, and I never fire at a target I don't have a visual on."

"That's good practice. You have a concealed carry permit?"

"Yes, and a permit for the Glock I'm carrying. Both are in my wallet."

"We'll take a look at them down at the station."

"You're taking him to the sheriff's office?" Wren cut in. "Why?"

"Because he is the sole witness, and I want to make sure I get the facts right. We'll record your statement. I have the equipment to do that there."

"I'll follow you over." He fished keys from his pocket, but she shook her head.

"How about I drive you there and back?" She smiled. "You can sit in the front."

"That's generous of you, Deputy Simmons," he said with just enough of a wry edge in his voice to make her chuckle.

"I always liked you. You know that? Even when you were being a giant pain in my behind."

"When was I ever that?"

"I'll rephrase the comment," she replied. "Even when the people in this town were being giant pains in my behind, calling me every other night to report the fact that you existed, I liked you. Come on. Let's get this done. I want to get back here in time to see how the newbie does collecting evidence in the apartment."

"I think I had better take charge of that," Levi said.

"Supervise him? Sure. Take charge of? I think he will learn better if he does it himself. Make sure all the surfaces are checked for prints. The more evidence we collect, the tighter our case will be when we find this guy."

"Do you want me to go to the station with them, Wren?" Annalise asked, hurrying down the porch steps.

"I don't need a lawyer," Titus replied before Wren could. He'd rather Annalise and Radley stayed with her. She needed the support a lot more than he did.

"That's what most people say right before they realize they do." Annalise brushed a few pieces of lint from her suit jacket. "It's your call, Wren. I'm here, so I may as well work."

"That's probably a good idea," Wren said. "I'll take Deputy Goodwin and Deputy...?"

"Henry. Deputy Brock Henry."

"Right. I'll take you to the apartment. I'm assuming Radley will join us there soon." She glanced at the road and frowned. "Maybe we should call and check in with him."

"If you're talking about the FBI agent who is down by the beach access road, he's with the sheriff. They'll be here as soon as they finish processing the scene."

"Then, I guess that settles it," Annalise said. "I'll grab my purse and head to the station. I'll see you both there." She speared Deputy Simmons with a hard look. "Remember, my client has a right to refuse to answer your questions without me present."

Hannah scowled, her eyes narrowing. "I'm not sure who you think you are, Ms.—"

"Special Agent Annalise Rivers. I'm an

attorney with the Federal Bureau of Investigation." She offered a hand, and Hannah shook it.

"Right. Well, here is who I am—a small-town deputy who believes in being honest and forthright about my intentions. If I planned to charge Titus with anything, he would know it. Since he hasn't committed a crime, I have no reason to. But feel free to waste your time." She shrugged. "Let's head out."

She strode across the yard and climbed into her vehicle without another word.

"That went well," Annalise murmured, smoothing her hand over perfectly styled hair and then down the front of her jacket.

"You're a bulldog in the courtroom, Anna," Wren replied. "But it's okay to approach things with a little more diplomacy out on the street." She smiled to take the sting out of the words, then met Titus's eyes. "I suggest you do what Annalise tells you. She knows how to keep innocent people out of trouble. I'm heading

over to the apartment. If you need anything, you can reach me through Radley.
You have his number?"

"Yes."

"I'll pick you up a prepaid phone while
I'm in town," Annalise said. "Since the
sheriff is keeping yours for no apparent
reason."

"It's evidence," Levi offered, but Annalise wasn't interested in listening. She
was walking across the yard, heading toward her SUV.

"You'd better head out," Wren said. She
was looking into Titus's eyes again. There
were flecks of gold in the depths of her
nearly black irises, and he found himself
lost in her gaze, searching for hints of
what they had once been to each other.

Best of friends.

Closest allies.

Always ready to go to battle for one another.

Whether she realized it or not, she had
jumped back into that role when she'd

agreed that Annalise should go to the sheriff's office with him.

"Before Deputy Simmons starts honking the horn at me?"

"And changes her mind about letting you sit in the front." She grinned, the amusement in her eyes making him want to pull her in for the kind of hug they had offered each other dozens of times before.

He didn't want to chase the smile from her face, so he kept his distance, watching as the smile faded and her eyes became somber. "You really do need to go."

"I know, but if you need me, all you have to do is call."

He had spoken those same words the morning of his wedding. Wren had stood in the place of best man, helping with his tux and straightening his tie and assuring him that the day would go off without a hitch. If she'd had reservations about Meghan, she hadn't let on. From the moment he had told her he planned to propose until the day he had accused her of lying out of jealousy and spite, Wren had never been anything but supportive of his relationship.

That day, she had smiled and laughed and joked and acted as if she completely approved of his choice of brides. Maybe she had. He had never asked. He had been too consumed by his desire for Meghan and too caught up in the idea of marriage and family.

She frowned. "Don't say things you don't mean, Titus."

"I mean them. I meant them."

Her frown deepened, and she shook her head. "I'm going to the apartment. I'll see you when you get back."

She walked away, and both deputies followed.

He had no choice but to climb into Deputy Simmons's car and head to the sheriff's office.

"You two give up on your friendship?" she asked as she put the vehicle into Drive.

"Wren and I?"

"I'm not talking about you and Levi, that's for sure."

"We haven't spoken in a few years. This is the first time I've seen her since I moved back to town."

"That's a shame. You two made a good couple."

"We were never a couple."

"Well, maybe you should have been. Listen, there's a reason I wanted you to ride along with me, and it wasn't just to save you wear and tear on your vehicle."

"What's that?"

"Something fishy is going on in this town. I can't put my finger on what."

"Fishy?"

"Every person that I know who's older than seventy is suddenly keen to sell mort-gage-free property to buy a place in the retirement village."

"People get older. They start needing a little more help."

"That's hogwash. The people I'm talking about could live independently for another ten or fifteen years."

"That's happening all over the country, Deputy Simmons."

"Call me Hannah. And, sure it is, but not at this rate. We're talking people who have sworn up and down that they'll never move, and three weeks later they're putting for-sale signs up in front of their houses."

"Even if they're being talked into it, that's not a crime. Which I'm sure you know."

"I do, and that's not the reason I wanted to speak with you alone."

"Then what is?"

"I'm not sure what happened to Abigail was an accident."

"What are you talking about?"

"Her broken hip. She was found at the bottom of her stairs by a concerned church member. She hadn't shown up for church."

"She's eighty-two. People her age do fall, and they do break bones."

"She said she was pushed, Titus. That's what she told the person who found her, and it's what she told the doctors."

His blood ran cold at the words. "Did the sheriff's department investigate?"

"We did, but Abigail also had a head injury. It could have been caused by the fall or by a blunt force object. The sheriff questioned her, and she changed her story, said that she had been mistaken. She wasn't pushed, she lost her footing on a loose carpet tread."

"Does Wren know this?"

"I didn't tell her. The sheriff marked the case as closed, and I've got no business going around stirring up trouble."

"But, you're telling me."

"Because the retirement village has a historical home on the property. The investment firm that bought the land had to agree to leave it right where it is. They can sell it if they want, but they can't tear it down and they can't move it."

"And?"

"It's been eight years since the land was sold, and they've done nothing with the house. I'm assuming they're trying to let time and weather do what the bylaws of the community won't allow."

"Destroy the house?"

"Right. But if a concerned citizen happened to lodge a complaint, we would have good reason to pay the retirement village a visit."

"I'm assuming you want me to be the concerned citizen?"

"You're the historical property restoration expert, and you know someone who is planning to move there. You can say that you were there touring the property and happened to notice the state of disrepair."

"I don't lie, Hannah."

"Okay. Then ask Wren to take you for the tour. After that, call the historic society and the town council."

"Is there a reason why you're not doing that?"

"As a member of the sheriff's department, it's important that I remain neutral."

"You could send an anonymous tip."

"The sheriff would know it was me. I've been talking about the place for months, wondering what's going on behind the manicured lawns and beautiful facade. The sheriff's mother lives there. He says it's all on the up-and-up and I need to leave it alone, but I believe in going with my gut. My gut says there's something going on there. My brain says I don't need to lose my job when I have two kids still in college and a husband on disability."

"You think whatever is happening here has something to do with Ryan's murder?"

She was silent for several heartbeats, her gaze focused on the road, her hands firm on the steering wheel. She had six children. Three still live at home. Her husband had been diagnosed with multiple sclerosis a few months after Titus returned. He thought she was probably in her midfifties, closing in on early retirement but unable to leave her job because she had too many people depending on her. "I don't know, but I'm worried enough to want to have a reason to go check things out."

"If I find the historical home needs work, I'll contact the town council and file a complaint with your department."

"So you're going to do it?"

"After all the trouble I put you through when I was a kid, I don't think I have much of a choice. I owe you."

"The town put me through the trouble. You were never a problem." She pulled into the parking lot on the south side of the sheriff's department and parked.

"Remember, this is our secret."

"I'm not much better with secrets than I am with lies," he responded. He had spent too much of his childhood carrying his mother's secrets. Her addictions had been a well-known fact in the community, but he had never spoken of them. When his mother had failed to show up for parent-teacher conferences, he had always lied about the reason.

"Me, neither, but something is going on in this town, and whatever it is might be the reason Ryan was killed. I'd hate to be next. What about you?" She speared him with a hard look and got out of the vehicle. "Come on. Let's get this over with. I need to get back to the farm so I can supervise the new kid and Levi."

"Levi has been a deputy for a while," he pointed out, following her across the parking lot to a locked door at the side of the building.

"Six years. He's a good guy. I like him, but he doesn't always think for himself. Sometimes, he needs a nudge to do the job the right way."

"And your way is the right way?"

She took keys from her pocket and unlocked the door.

"No, the right way is the way that will preserve the crime scene and ensure that we didn't miss anything. We don't have a lot of crime in Hidden Cove. When we do, it's important that we process things correctly. I'd hate for a guilty man or woman to walk free in this town because of a mistake we made."

"I'm sure the town feels the same way."

"Right, and I'm being paid to do a job. I'm going to do it to the best of my ability. I don't care who ends up in the crosshairs of my investigation."

He wanted to ask what she meant—*who* she meant—but two deputies were walking through the corridor. He might not be big on secrets, but he could keep them when it was necessary. He didn't know what was going on. He had no idea what might be happening at Sunrise Acres Retirement Village. Until he figured it out, Hannah's secret was safe with him.

SEVEN

By the time Radley and the sheriff returned to the farmhouse, Wren had already walked through the apartment with Levi and Brock. They had dusted every surface for prints, done a thorough search for evidence and then called it good.

She was satisfied with that.

As a law enforcement officer, she knew how difficult it was to prioritize a crime like this. Breaking and entering, theft and vandalism—they were not high priority. Even in a place like Hidden Cove where the crime rate was low and the docket of open cases small, breaking and entering wasn't a crime that received a whole lot of attention.

She didn't mind that.

What bothered her was the sheriff.

He hadn't gone to the apartment, hadn't looked inside, hadn't given any indication that he thought the crime was related to Ryan's murder and the fire. He stood with his arms crossed over his chest, his dark uniform speckled with the first drops of rain. There hadn't been a downpour yet, but she was expecting one.

"It seems to me we're getting a lot of callouts for your family," the sheriff said, his gaze boring into hers. She wasn't sure if he was trying to intimidate her or read guilt in her expression.

"You're getting calls because my family is being targeted by someone," she responded, meeting his gaze without flinching or looking away. She had been in law enforcement for over a decade. She knew how to deal with men like him.

"Who?" He snapped the one-word question, trying to throw her off her stride and make her slip.

A good strategy for interrogating a suspect. Unless the suspect was innocent.

Wren was. She had nothing to hide. No reason to not answer his questions. "I have no idea. It's your office's job to find out. Maybe you should spend more time doing that, and less time interrogating innocent people."

He scowled. "The fact that you're an FBI agent does not give you the right to come to this town and tell me how to run my office."

"I don't recall telling you anything. You asked me questions. I was giving you answers appropriate to them. If you want to discuss the handling of this case, you are better off doing that with your deputies. I have a funeral to plan."

"I know." He sighed. "And I'm not trying to make life more difficult during this already difficult time. I'm just trying to find answers, and everything that is happening centers around you and your family. Is it possible someone from your past is coming after you?"

"You're talking about revenge for something involving my job?"

"Yes."

"If that were the case, why ransack Ryan's apartment?" she asked, bracing herself for whatever was coming next. She didn't believe the sheriff had suddenly forgotten that she was his prime suspect in Ryan's murder.

"To draw you out of the house and make you an easier target?"

"I wouldn't have known the perp had been in there if Titus hadn't seen him leaving."

The sheriff nodded. "I'm not ruling your job out as a reason for this, but it may be a stretch to think the break-in at the apartment is connected."

"Was it a break-in? I didn't see any evidence of lock tampering. The door hadn't been kicked in. I assumed the person who entered either had the key or found it unlocked."

She expected that to get his dander up.

She didn't know much about the sheriff, but she had heard stories about his gung ho approach to law enforcement. He believed in laying down the law with a heavy hand and little sympathy. If you committed a crime in Hidden Cove, you could expect to go to jail for it, no matter the circumstances.

The sheriff glanced at his deputies. They both shook their heads. "Apparently not. Who had the key? Aside from Ryan?"

"Abby kept a spare on her key ring. It's in a drawer in the kitchen. There's also a spare in the plotted plant to the left of the garage."

"Did you look to see if it was still there?"

"No."

"I will," Brock offered eagerly.

"Great. Meet us inside," the sheriff ordered.

He cupped Wren's elbow and began walking up the porch stairs.

She pulled free. "I'm steady on my feet,

Sheriff. There's no need for the support, but thanks."

"You can call me Camden. We did go to school together."

"If I remember correctly, you were a few years ahead of me."

"I was, but you were pretty unforgettable."

"Because I was always getting into trouble," she said, uncomfortable with the personal tone of the conversation. She met Radley's eyes. He looked as confused as she felt.

"Because you were smart."

"There were a lot of smart kids in my graduating class."

"Yeah, but you were the only one of them who was in my advanced chemistry class." He stopped at the door. She had no intention of opening it. He had already been inside and helped process the scene there.

"Does this have anything to do with what happened to Ryan?" she asked, determined to get the conversation back on more neutral ground.

"Just making friendly conversation, trying to put you at ease."

"Thinking about the past doesn't put me at ease. Solving cases does."

"Right. Well, as we've established, this is my jurisdiction. I don't need help solving cases here, and the best thing you can do to help us find Ryan's killer is be completely honest with me."

"I have been."

"There was no gun residue on your hands, Wren. There was no blood splatter on your clothes. We both know that doesn't necessarily mean you're innocent."

"I was kidnapped by two men in police uniforms who were driving a marked police car. Why would I go through that just to convince you that I didn't kill Ryan?"

"Because a victim isn't always looked at as a suspect. Not at first."

"What's your point, Camden?"

"No one saw the police vehicle or the officers. Except you."

"I was handcuffed."

"You have handcuffs. It's part of your job."

"Someone shot at me and Titus. So there's your witness," she replied.

"He's a good friend of yours."

"He was. We haven't spoken in years, and you and I have already been through this. There's no reason to keep me on your suspect list, but if you want to waste your time, that's your business. The apartment has been processed, and I'm going to clean it. If you need me, you know where to find me."

She didn't give him a chance to respond.

The house was a mess. Abigail was fighting to get the doctor to release her early from rehab. She couldn't return to this mess.

"Do you want some help?" Radley asked.

"Can you call the field office? Ask the tech people to do some research on these two properties." She pulled the brochures from her pocket and handed them to him.

"What properties?" the sheriff asked, stepping closer and eyeing the brochures.

Radley tucked them in his suit pocket. "Anything in particular you want to know?"

"How long they've been in existence? Who owns them? What other investments they're involved in."

"If they're legitimate?" he suggested.

"That, too."

"I'll get it done." He walked back into the house.

Cleaning the house would require scrubbing soot from floors and walls. It would probably require paint and ladders and equipment that she couldn't manage with one good arm. She went to the apartment, ignoring the sheriff and deputies, who were watching her. The door was still open a crack and she stepped in, closing it firmly and locking it.

There were layers of dusting powder on every surface and trash everywhere. If there was one thing she had learned as a child, it was that keeping busy and active could help keep the brain focused on things other than whatever trauma or trouble was happening.

She grabbed large trash bags from under the sink and began filling them. It was a slow process, her injured arm in the sling and held close to her chest, but slow progress was still progress. If she kept at it long enough, she would get the job done. The words of Abigail's favorite hymn drifted through her mind.

"'It is well with my soul,'" she whispered as she scooped up stuffing that was strewn across the floor. There were pieces of Ryan's life mixed with the detritus scattered across the room. Shirts that had been tossed from the small dresser. Shorts and jeans she could remember him wearing. Papers with his handwriting on them.

"'It is well with my soul,'" she repeated.

Still, her soul didn't feel well. It felt disquieted and unsettled, her heart aching with the finality of Ryan's death. He was gone. She had watched him fall, seen the blood spurting from his chest. She had known that he would die no matter how frantically she tried to save him.

"I'm so sorry, Ryan." Her voice broke and tears slid down her cheek. They continued to fall as she tossed more trash in the bag. Despite being one-armed and exhausted, she couldn't leave the job for someone else. This was Ryan's space, and she wanted to make sure nothing got thrown out that he would have wanted to be kept.

Not that he had much.

His entire life had been crammed into the efficiency. He had left his furniture, books and music equipment at the house that had been foreclosed on. Aside from clothes and a few personal items, the only thing he'd brought was his Fender acoustic guitar.

She was puzzled.

She hadn't seen it when she'd walked through earlier. Usually it was displayed in a corner near the couch, the glossy finish gleaming. Ryan had played it nearly every day, often picking it up and strumming it while they talked.

Which hadn't been often enough.

As much as she had loved him, they had been very different people. She wished she had made more of an effort to connect with him and to learn more about the man he had become.

She wiped tears from her cheeks and carried a filled bag to the front door. Her broken wrist ached, and she told herself that was why the tears were flowing so easily. She didn't like crying, and she didn't enjoy feeling weak. She couldn't seem to stop the tears, and her body wanted nothing more than a few hours of sleep.

She filled two more bags, the tears finally drying as she opened the door and set all three on the stoop. She would take them down to the garage when she was finished and put them in the garbage bin there. First, though, she wanted to finish.

And find the guitar.

"Wren?"

She heard the voice seconds before she closed the door.

She wanted to pretend she hadn't because she knew who it belonged to, but Abigail had trained most of the rudeness out of her.

She reopened the door, watching as Titus took the stairs two at a time, his dark hair speckled with drops of frozen rain.

She hadn't realized the storm had arrived.

Now she could hear the patter of ice on the roof and the awning above the landing.

"How did it go?" she asked, determined to be polite and friendly. Despite their past, she had no reason to give him the cold shoulder or—as he had called it— run away.

"Pretty much what I expected." He glanced down the stairs, and waved at the sheriff and Deputy Simmons. "Doing some cleaning up?"

"Yes."

"I'll give you a hand." He walked into the apartment before she could protest.

She followed, closing the door against the cold before turning to face him.

He had already grabbed a trash bag and was filling it.

"Titus, I can manage on my own."

"Of course you can."

"What I'm saying is that I don't need your help."

"What you're saying is that you don't *want* my help," he corrected as he shoved a disemboweled pillow into the bag. "Or that you don't want me here."

"I didn't say either of those things."

But they were both true.

He studied her face, tracing a line from her eyes to her lips with his gaze. She refused to look away, and she refused to blush. "What?" she asked.

"Is it because you've been crying?"

"Who said I've been crying?" she responded, grabbing a bag from the box and walking to the kitchen area with it.

"You." He followed her and traced a line from the corner of her eye to her jaw with his finger.

"I saw him get shot, and I watched him die," she said, her voice husky with emotion. "If that's not a reason to cry, I don't know what is."

"You have every reason to cry and no reason to be embarrassed by it."

"I'm not embarrassed." She reached for a trash can that had been turned upside down and righted it, grabbing a few papers that spilled out next to it.

"Then...you just don't want me around?"

"Titus, I'm not sure what this conversation is about, but if it's not about Ryan's murder and everything else that has happened in the last twenty-four hours, I really don't have time for it."

She sounded harsh and rude, and she regretted it immediately.

"I'm sorry," she murmured. "That sounded a lot ruder than I meant it."

She tossed the papers into the trash bag and grabbed an empty sack that had once been filled with flour.

"That's one of the things I've always admired about you," Titus said.

She met his eyes, saw the tenderness in his eyes and in his face. He had looked at her that way the night she had found out her high school sweetheart had cheated. It was the way he had looked at their senior prom when they had decided to dance one dance together because their favorite slow song was playing and their dates were chatting with friends.

She had fallen in love with him that night. And she had fallen hard.

She had never told him that. She had barely wanted to admit it to herself, but the puppy love that had begun when they were in middle school had morphed into something that had felt deep and very real.

"What?" she said, wanting to step out of

the tiny alcove kitchen and into the larger room. Unfortunately, that would mean brushing past Titus, and if she touched him, all the memories of bear hugs and whispered secrets might make her stop and reach for him. She might step into his arms the way she had when they were kids trying to be there for each other in the most platonic and friendly of ways.

"Even when we were kids, you were never afraid to admit when you were wrong, and you were always quick to apologize."

She shrugged, trying not to shift uncomfortably. "Lots of people are capable of admitting when they're wrong and apologizing."

"Maybe so, but it always struck me as a great quality. There were other things that weren't so great."

"I guess you're about to tell me which ones," she said.

He took a step closer and cupped her jaw with both hands. His skin was warm and callused, his touch light and gentle. "Just one. You always had a difficult time accepting apologies from other people, and you held on to hurts for a very long time. As a matter of fact, I'm not sure you ever let them go."

"I was serious when I said I didn't have time for conversations that weren't about the case."

"I'm getting there," he responded, his gaze dropping to her lips.

"Titus..."

She wasn't sure what she intended to say. Maybe she planned to ask him to move out of her way so that she could breathe again.

Then his hands slipped from her face to her shoulders, his warmth seeping through her shirt.

When he pulled her into his chest, she went willingly, her head finding the spot right beneath his chin, her uninjured arm sliding around his lean waist. It felt good to be there. Like returning home after a long absence. And she didn't want to leave again, so she allowed herself to relax against him, to let his arms slide down her back, his hands settle on her lower spine.

She inhaled the spicy fragrance of his soap and the clean linen scent of his clothes. She wanted more than anything to let herself drift for a while and forget all the heartache of the day.

"I'm sorry, Wren. For the hurt I caused you, for accusing you of things I should have known weren't true. More than anything, I'm sorry for the years we lost because of it. I know it's not your habit to give people second chances, but I want one with you. The second chance. The fresh start. The friendship we should have always had, rebuilt into something stronger."

His words enveloped her—as warm and comforting as his touch.

He was right. She didn't believe in giving people who had hurt her second chances. She had watched her mother do that so many times it had killed her.

But this was Titus. Her best childhood friend.

Cutting ties with the person who knew her best had been difficult. She had mourned the loss for weeks. After that, she had picked herself up, brushed herself off and gone on with her life.

Now she was back in his arms, listening to his heartbeat, remembering how much fun their friendship had been, how comforting and inviting and lovely, and she wondered if they could revisit it. If it might be possible to go back to that comfortable and comforting relationship.

If it was, would she want to?

Could she give Titus the second chance she had never offered anyone else?

"Do you think it's possible?" Titus whispered, his breath tickling her ear.

"Maybe," she said. "Probably."

"That's better than no," he replied, easing back and looking into her face. "I need to go out to Sunrise Acres Retirement Village tomorrow. Will you go with me?"

"Does it have something to do with what happened to Ryan?" she asked, stepping out of his arms and tossing a few more pieces of trash into the bag.

"It may."

"Really?" She met his eyes, intrigued. "How so?"

"Hannah Simmons asked me to check things out for her."

"What things?"

"She says she has a bad feeling about the place."

"Why doesn't she go to the sheriff?"

"She tried. He's not very open to her."

"All right. I'll go. What time?"

"The office opens at eight. I'd like to be there then. I'm hoping we can talk them into giving us a tour of the property."

"I'll call and make the arrangements. Since Abigail is buying a place there, they should be eager to arrange a tour for us."

"Great. Let's get this cleaned up, and

then we'll head over to the house. I'll tell you about my plans for it." He smiled, and she couldn't help smiling in return.

Cleaning the apartment had taken several hours. Explaining his plans for restoring the farmhouse took almost another one. By the time Titus had left the farm, it had been early evening, the road slick with a layer of melting ice and slush. As soon as he had returned home, he had typed up his plan for the farmhouse, put together an estimate and slashed everything off the cost except materials that he knew he didn't already have in stock. He kept a shed filled with reclaimed floorboards, railings, doors, windows and hardware. He planned to donate as much as he could to the project. He would have donated everything if he had thought Abigail would agree to it. He had put the plan in a folder and left it on the desk in his office, then spent the remainder of the evening working up estimates for two other clients. One owned an 1890s Victorian with water views. The other had a shotgun-style bungalow on Main Street. Both would be total restorations, and both were projects he was looking forward to. He had enjoyed his time as police officer in Boston. He had worked his way up to detective, and he had enjoyed his job.

But this? It was what he felt like he was meant to do. He might have complained about small-town life when he was a kid, but he'd learned to enjoy the slower pace of life, the strong sense of community, the deep ties that bound the residents of Hidden Cove together.

He couldn't imagine going back to Boston.

God's plans were best. He had always believed that They were also often unexpected and unanticipated.

Five years after the retirement party, Titus could see the fruit of his faith in the thriving business he had taken over and was building on. Moving back to Hidden Cove had been the right decision.

Still, at nearly five in the morning, as he brewed coffee in the immaculate kitchen and listened to rain falling on the tin roof of the old bungalow, he couldn't help wishing he had someone to share the quiet hours with, someone to share coffee and eggs and toast with.

Someone to share life with.

He hadn't imagined growing old alone in the house he had spent so many difficult years in. He had made a good life for himself, but there were moments when he felt an unexpected pang of loneliness.

His phone rang as he took eggs from the refrigerator.

He answered quickly, certain it was bad news. No one called with good news this time of the morning.

"Hello?"

"Titus? It's Wren. I couldn't sleep and decided to head over to the Sunrise Acres."

"At five in the morning?" He poured coffee into a mug and cracked several eggs into a bowl.

"I thought we could stop and see Abby first."

"I'll repeat my question. At five in the morning?"

"I'll repeat my original comment—I couldn't sleep."

"I see. You figured you would wake Abby up so the three of us could be wide awake before dawn together?" he asked, hoping to make her laugh.

"She's always an early riser. Even during rehab, she's always up before dawn. Besides, I want to ask her about the brochures we found. There has to be a reason they were in the attic."

"Were your people able to find any information about the investment company?"

"Radley sent the information to the Boston field office. We have some people researching it. So far, nothing has come up. The company seems to be legitimate. They'll dig a little deeper, but I'm not counting on getting answers there."

"So you're going to Abby."

"I can't go to Ryan. So, yes." He thought her voice cracked. It reminded him of her tear-streaked face and red-rimmed eyes, and the way it had felt to hold her in his arms.

She had always been his buddy and pal, his companion and troublemaking partner. They had gone on hundreds of adventures when they were young, exploring the cove and the surrounding area until they knew it as well as they knew their names. In all that time, he had never wondered what it would be like to be more than friends. He hadn't considered crossing the invisible line that separated friendship from something more.

Yesterday, though, he had felt something unexpected when he had hugged her. Attraction. Chemistry. Longing. Things that he never would have put in a sentence with Wren's name.

"Are you okay?" he asked, wishing she was in the room with him so that he could see her face and read her expression.

"Fine. Just anxious to get started with the day. The more we investigate, the closer it will bring us to the truth."

"I just need to throw on some shoes, so I'm ready when you are," he said, grabbing shoes from the rack near the door.

"I'm ready."

"What's your ETA?"

"It's 0515."

He glanced at the clock on the stove. "That's the current time."

"I know. I'm parked in your driveway. I pulled in about twenty minutes ago and waited until I saw a light go on."

"That was very thoughtful of you," he said wryly.

She laughed, the warmth of it drifting through the phone. "Every once in a while, I try to be that."

"Thoughtful?"

"Yes."

"You always are. How about you come in for a minute. I'm making eggs.

"I'm not hungry."

"I am."

"Fine, but I have Radley and Annalise with me."

"You woke them up for your early morning adventures?"

"No, they woke themselves up and insisted on coming."

"All right. Bring them in. I'll unlock the front door. No need to knock. We'll leave after we eat."

He hung up, added the remainder of the eggs to the bowl, grabbed bread to toast and waited for Wren and her entourage to join him. They had a lot of ground to cover and a lot of questions that needed to be answered. Ryan's murderer needed to be apprehended, and the first step to accomplishing that was understanding what he had been involved in before his death.

That and keeping Wren safe were Titus's top priorities.

There would be time for exploring the boundaries of his relationship with Wren after those two goals had been accom-

plished. He believed that. Just as he believed that God would see them through
this newest challenge the way He had the
other ones they had faced—with strength
and grace and courage.

One step at a time.

They would reach the end of this, and
then, he hoped, they could begin something new and wonderful.

EIGHT

Wren had forgotten what a good cook Titus was.

She had also forgotten how charming he could be, the way he looked straight into people's eyes when he spoke and gave all his attention to the person he was conversing with. He never seemed distracted or in a hurry.

She had watched him while he made eggs and toast and served coffee, and all the little things she hadn't thought about in years had come back. He had been the cook because his mother hadn't cared about eating. He had learned to be charming because often he'd had to talk bill collectors out of turning off utilities. The rest—the focus and interest and intensity—she assumed he had taught himself in order to not be like his mother.

Wren had only had a couple of conversations with her. She had usually been too drunk or too stoned to be even realize there was company in the house. Wren and Titus would grab what snacks or drinks they could scrounge up and go explore the creek and forest. His mother had never asked when he would be back. She had never checked on them. Even in the worst weather, she had never told them not to go.

Obviously, her absentee parenting had affected Titus. It wasn't something they had ever discussed. They had been too busy planning adventures and talking about their futures to discuss the state of his home life.

She watched him as he pulled through the gates that led into Sunrise Acres Retirement Village. They had already visited Abigail. She hadn't recognized the brochures and had no idea why they had been in the attic over the garage.

Which left Ryan as the person who had put them there.

And he wasn't around to answer their questions.

"You've been quiet this morning," Titus commented as he parked near the community center, which housed the main office and reception area.

"I have a lot on my mind." She glanced out the window, watching as Annalise pulled into the spot beside them. Radley was in the passenger seat, staring glumly at the building. He would rather be working a case in Boston and spending time with his wife and baby daughter. The fact that he was here meant a lot to her.

"Anything I can help with?"

"Not unless you know who killed Ryan and can point your finger in his direction."

"I wish I could," he said.

"If wishes were horses…"

"Beggars would ride. Abby always loved

saying that to us." He grinned, jumping out of the truck and coming around to open her door.

She could have managed herself.

They both knew it, but his smile when he looked into her eyes kept her from saying it. "Hopefully, this tour will give us some information we don't already have."

"Who is giving the tour?" he asked.

"Lester Thomas. He's the director of operations here."

"Bald? Short? A little...round? Wears fancy suits with wrinkled dress shirts."

She smiled at his description. "Obviously, you've met."

"He attends Hidden Cove Community Church. We've waved to each other a few times, but I don't recall ever having a conversation with him."

"He visited the hospital after Abigail's surgery."

"They're friends?"

"She met him when she did the tour with Ryan." Wren had been excluded from the plans and informed of the visit after the fact.

She hadn't been happy about it, but she hadn't told Abigail that. All she had been able to do was listen as Abigail gushed about the beautiful condos and cottages, the tennis court, the stunning gardens. Wren hadn't asked the cost or questioned the wisdom of selling a family property to purchase something new.

That hadn't been her right—she wasn't Abigail's daughter or granddaughter.

Nonetheless, she had thought about it a lot.

She had mentally questioned everything about the posh retirement village with the cove views and stunning ocean vistas.

"That's the only way they know each other? From a tour?" Titus asked incredulously.

"I was surprised, too, but according to Abigail, that's the case."

"We all set to head in?" Annalise asked, glancing at her watch and sliding a file folder into her leather messenger bag. "I have a conference call at ten, and I don't think this is the right place to do it."

"If you two want to head back to the farmhouse now—"

"No," Radley cut her off, his blue eyes flashing with irritation. "We didn't let you come here alone, and we aren't letting you wander around the property alone."

"I'm not alone."

"Obviously not," Radley said, his gaze dropping to Titus's hand.

It was still resting on Wren's lower back.

"Is something bothering you?" Titus asked easily, his hand staying exactly where it was.

Wren could have easily stepped away, but being close to him felt as natural as breathing. Maybe she should fight it. Maybe she should try not to reconnect with him. That had certainly been her intention when she had arrived bleeding on his doorstep.

But she had missed Titus. She had

missed *them*—two misfit kids against the world.

Only they weren't kids anymore.

They weren't misfits.

They were professionals making good lives for themselves, and she was curious to see how that changed the dynamic between them.

"This whole thing is bothering me," Radley replied, his focus turning to their surroundings. They were following a stone path to the front door. To their right, a ramp allowed wheelchair access to the clubhouse. "The investment firm that owns this property is on the up-and-up. There's no evidence of tax fraud, no bad checks or other criminal charges. I should be thinking things are fine, but I don't like the feel of this place."

"You don't like hospitals or rehab centers, either," Annalise pointed out. "I've had to visit you twice in each, and you spent most of our time asking me to get you out."

"Your point being?" Radley asked.

"Why wouldn't you have a bad feeling about a place like this? It's where people without families go to die."

"That's an interesting way to put it, but I wouldn't say it's accurate. There are plenty of people in retirement homes who have loving families. They move to retirement homes to free up time and energy so they can spend their later years enjoying themselves rather than keeping up on housework and yards," Titus said, pushing open the door that led into the clubhouse. The interior of the building was as beautiful as the exterior. Marble floor. Potted plants. A center staircase that curved to the left and right. Mahogany railing and bold oil paintings. The place had been decorated to look both opulent and inviting.

"Can I help you?" a woman called out from her seat behind a huge mahogany desk.

"We're meeting with Mr. Thomas. He's giving us a tour," Wren responded.

"You must be Wren Santino!" The

woman rounded the desk and shook Wren's hand as if she were a celebrity.

"That's correct. My foster mother—"

"Abigail Maccabee. I had a wonderful visit with her when she took the tour. I heard she'd broken her hip. Such a shame. Hopefully, she'll find a nice cottage or condo here to recover in once she's able to return home."

"How do you know she isn't home now?" Wren asked, studying the woman's face and trying to determine if she knew her. Midforties with perfect makeup and perfectly styled hair, she looked like she'd had at least one face-lift. It had tightened the skin around her eyes and plumped her lips to unnatural proportions.

"You know how small towns are," the woman said, her face going a deep shade of crimson. "People talk."

"Yes, they do, Ms...?"

"Alison Spindle. I'm the assistant manager of the facility," she said, her smile returning. "I've been here since it opened."

"And you like it?"

"Absolutely. Employees are given the option to live in. I opted for a condo with a view of the bay. It's breathtaking. You are, of course, in the clubhouse. This is where we host parties and dances, talent shows. We've even had a few weddings here." Her eyes sparkled as she went into detail about the couples who had met and married at Sunrise Acres.

"That's wonderful," Wren said, finally managing to cut into the woman's monologue. "Is Lester in? We have a busy schedule, and I don't want to be late for my next appointment."

"Yes. His office is this way. Just down the hall and around the corner. You can all come. I have to tell you, I was shocked to hear about Ryan's death. Just shocked. Is that why your schedule is packed? Dealing with the arrangements and everything?"

It was an oddly personal question, and Wren didn't have any intention of answering. "You knew Ryan?" she asked, certain the woman would be happy to continue talking.

"Knew him? Of course! He was nearly a fixture around here these past few months," she gushed. "He'd bring cupcakes or cookies from the bakery and hang around and chat after he met with Lester."

"Why did he meet with Lester?" Titus asked, and Alison blushed again.

"I'm really not sure. I thought it was something to do with Abigail moving here," she said.

Something about her tone made Wren think she was lying, that maybe she knew more than she was letting on.

"Here you are!" she said brightly, knocking on a door and opening it. "Lester, your appointment is here!" she announced, and then she offered a quick wave and jogged away.

"For someone who loves to talk, she sure was suddenly eager to escape," Titus whispered in Wren's ear as they stepped across the threshold.

The room beyond was as impressive as the lobby—dark wood floor, gleaming desk, picture windows that looked out over a beautiful yard and fountain.

Lester Thomas sat behind the desk, his spotless suit jacket thrown over a wrinkled purple shirt.

"Wren!" he exclaimed as she walked toward him. "It's so good to see you again! How is Abigail? The news about Ryan's death must have taken a toll on her." He clasped her hand, kissed her left cheek and then her right. Her skin crawled and she took a step back, pulling her hands from his.

His bright smile faded a little, his beady brown gaze darting from one person to the next. "Who are your friends? I didn't realize we were going to have such a large group."

"Is four people a large group?" Titus

asked, and Lester's smile dropped away completely.

"I had tea for two ordered. I'll have to call the kitchen and tell them we need three extra settings."

"There's no need for tea, Lester. I'm just here to tour the facility and the grounds."

"Abigail sent you?"

"She values my opinion," she responded, not willing to lie, but not wanting him to know the real reason she was there.

"I'm sure she does, but she and Ryan both loved Sunrise Acres. I thought she planned to sign the paperwork once she was released from rehab."

"Who told you that?"

"That was the implication I got the last time we met. Maybe I misread her. It's sometimes hard to know what a person really means. Let's get to the tour. We'll start here. In the clubhouse."

He led the way out of the room.

When Wren started following, Titus pulled her back, leaning down so his lips were against her ear. "Hannah was right. This place feels off."

"I agree."

"How about I split off from the group and see what I can dig up while you do the tour?"

"That is not a good idea."

"Why not?" he asked, turning her so they were face-to-face. He had his hands hooked around her waist, and if anyone came looking for them, they'd see a couple having a private conversation.

She knew that was his intention, but being in his arms made her pulse race and her thoughts fly away. If she had been braver, she would have told him that.

"Because we need to stick together," she managed to say, her voice thick with longing.

If he heard it, he didn't let on. He seemed focused on the goal of finding out what he could about Sunrise Acres Retirement Village.

"Because?" he pressed.

She had no answer to that. Just the knee-jerk feeling that something was very wrong in this posh and peaceful community.

"You two coming?" Radley appeared in the doorway, his blue eyes sharp with curiosity and concern.

"Yes," Wren replied, hurrying toward him.

"I have some things to take care of," Titus said. "I'll join you when I'm finished."

"Titus," she began, but Radley was watching and she really had no valid excuse to keep Titus close. "Don't get into any trouble."

"When have I ever done that?" he asked with a grin that made her heart jump.

"Just every day of your life when we were kids."

"True, but we're not kids anymore." The grin faded, and he moved toward her, tugging her close and pressing a gentle kiss to her forehead. "You have a cell phone?"

"Yes." Annalise had purchased a prepaid phone for Wren to use while she waited for hers to be cleared as evidence and returned by the police.

"And my number?"

"I did call you this morning," she reminded him, more amused than irritated by his antics. This was the Titus she knew— taking charge and going his own way.

"Call me when the tour is over. I'll meet you at the car."

He walked out of the room and down the hall, saying something to Lester as he passed.

"Hey, what's going on between you two?" Radley asked as they followed Lester down the hall.

"Nothing."

"It looked like something to me," he said.

"Do you have a problem with that?" she asked. No heat in her voice. Just a question. Several of the Special Crimes Unit members had found love these past few years. He was one of them. There was nothing going on between her and Titus, but if there was, she doubted he'd have anything negative to say about it.

"No. Just curious. Come on. Let's get this thing over with. This place gives me the heebie-jeebies."

He grabbed her good arm and tugged her into a near run as Lester opened a door at the end of the hall and walked through.

If there was anything underhanded going on at Sunrise Acres, the people who lived there didn't seem to know about it. Titus wandered the grounds for an hour, talking to everyone he saw, getting a feel for the community and the people who lived there.

Everyone seemed happy.

A few mentioned a funeral they had been to the previous week. Stan Reginald had died suddenly in his sleep. A heart attack according to the coroner. His wife had found him in bed when she returned home from her morning walk with the girls. *The girls* being a group of women who walked the mile loop around a pond near the old house Titus was searching for.

He got directions to it and headed down a paved path that led through the garden. His phone buzzed as he reached the pond. The house was straight across the pristine water. He noted once-white clapboard siding gray with age and rot, shingles missing from the roof, the porch railing listing. A window in the attic was shattered. One on the second floor had a crack in it. The gingerbread trim had pieces missing.

Hannah was right. The place needed some serious work.

He glanced at the text message: Done. Finally. Meet me at the truck when you're ready.

He responded with a photo of the house and a simple question: Want to explore?

Absolutely, she replied, the text coming in quickly. He could almost feel her excitement. Like Titus, Wren had always love exploring. They had spent hours learning the woods surrounding his mother's property. They'd been in the old caves on the southern edge of the cove but had never seen this house. Back then, the land Sunrise Acres was built on had been thickly wooded and very difficult to access. Now it was lush lawns and beautiful ponds and cute cottage and condos that overlooked the water.

"Titus!" Wren called, and he turned toward her voice, smiling as she ran toward him. She had a lean build, long legs and a physique that would have been well suited to the Paris runway. She had never seemed to notice her beauty. Nor had she ever dressed to show off her delicate figure.

She had been a tomboy through and through. Eager to see the world and to tackle it with enthusiasm and passion.

"How was the tour? And where are your buddies?" he asked, taking her arm and pulling her into his side. She fit perfectly there, her body melting against his for a moment before she stiffened and pulled away.

"Maybe this isn't a good idea," she murmured, smoothing hair that she had tied into a tight bun at the base of her skull.

"Exploring that house? I think it's a great idea."

"You know that isn't what I'm talking about," she replied. "We are not a good idea. Us together is not a good idea. Hugs and standing close enough to touch. That is not a good idea."

"Why not?" he asked as they walked the path around the pond. The sun had risen high above their heads, the golden rays reflecting on the blue water.

"I could give you a lot of reasons that are partially true. I have a job in Boston. You work here. Old friendships may be the best friendships, but ours ended on a sour note, and it's probably best to leave it where it was. But the real reason is that I could get very close to you if I let myself. I could learn to trust you, and maybe learn to love you again."

"Again?" He pulled her to a stop and

searched her face for some sign that she was joking. She had an austere look that some people found off-putting. He had always found it intriguing. Now her expression was carefully hidden by a facade of indifference.

"You're saying you never knew?"

"Knew what, Wren? We were friends."

"I fell for you the night of our prom. When we danced together. I stood in your arms, and I only ever felt truly safe when I was with you. That was a heady feeling for someone like me." She smiled, but there was sadness in her eyes. Regret. Maybe a hint of self-deprecation.

"You never told me," he said, remembering that night and that moment. The way it had felt to look into her eyes. The tiny spark of recognition that had simmered in his heart. He had felt something, but he wouldn't have put the word *love* to it. He had been too young, too brash, to excited to step into the future and see what it brought.

"And ruin what we had?" she responded. "Why would I do that? I loved you as a friend first, and then I thought I loved you as more."

"Thought?"

She shrugged, her dark jacket clinging to her shoulders, her casted arm still in the sling and just peeking out from behind the fabric. "Who knows? It was a long time ago. We were teenagers. It was prom. It's possible I was swept away in the moment, but I don't want to be swept away again, and I think it could happen. I think if I spend too much time with you, if I touch your hand one too many times, or hug you or look into your eyes, that feeling might come back."

"And that would be a bad thing?"

"I don't know what it would be, but love has always led to me being hurt. That's what I know, and that's what I don't want."

"I would never intentionally hurt you, Wren. I hope you know that," he said, his hands sliding to her shoulders and skimming up the slim column of her throat, his palms resting near her jaw.

"I know you would never mean to hurt me," she replied, her eyes so sad his heart ached for her and for what he had unwittingly done—not just destroyed their friendship but also broken her heart.

"I'm sorry," he said, knowing it would never be enough.

"Of course, you are. You're a good guy. I never would have loved someone who wasn't."

"What about that geek from high school? And the guy from college?" he said, hoping to lighten the mood and draw some of the sadness from her eyes.

"That wasn't love. It was infatuation. What I felt for you…was different."

"I'm an idiot," he said. "Obviously. I could have married the perfect woman for me. Instead, I turned a blind eye and walked away."

"The perfect woman for you?" She

shook her head and smiled. "I used to drive you crazy."

"Yes, you did. In a good way. Remember when you got sent to the principal's office for intervening in a fight before school, and you sent an SOS via Andrea Danvers, saying you needed me to get in touch with Abigail so she could bail you out?"

"I'd forgotten about that." She started walking, her shoulders straight, her stride long, a smile still in place.

"Right. I had to fake a stomachache so I could go to the school nurse and use the phone. Of course, old Nurse Ratched—"

"Ms. Stanford was a lovely woman and a good nurse."

"She wanted to watch me toss my cookies before she let me use the phone. I tried to go in the bathroom and fake it, and that woman followed me in."

"You never told me that," she said, chuckling quietly.

She looked so beautiful in the sunlight, laughter softening her face, that he pulled her close and kissed her gently. Her lips were velvety soft beneath his, her body relaxed with laughter.

And that kiss, that moment, felt like one of the most right things he had ever done.

She pulled back, her eyes wide with surprise. "What was that?"

"You're beautiful in the sunlight," he said honestly.

"I just told you that I couldn't let this happen, Titus. I just said that I didn't want my heart to be broken again." She suddenly looked panicked. Nothing like the tough young woman he had known.

"Wren—"

"Don't!" She put her hand up. "I don't want to discuss it. Not now."

"Then when? Because you know that we *will* discuss it."

"Eventually. Right now, I want to go into the house and explore." She jogged away.

He followed silently, standing back just enough to give her space as she tried the door. "It's unlocked," she said almost gleefully.

"Then let's explore," he replied.

She smiled, but there was still tension in her face, her smile tight and a little brittle.

"Let's." She stepped into the house, and he followed, barreling into her back when she stopped short. His arms wrapped around her to keep her from falling, but she didn't seem to notice. She was staring into a room that opened to the left of the foyer.

"Oh no," she said.

"What?" he asked, and then he saw it.

A leg.

And then the body it was attached to.

Shocked, he ran into the room, Wren right behind him. He knew what he was seeing, but he couldn't seem to wrap his mind around it. Hannah Simmons was lying on the floor. Dead.

He was almost certain of it, but he sprinted across the room, dropped down beside her and felt for a pulse, praying desperately that he would find one.

NINE

Hannah Simmons was dead.

Wren couldn't wrap her mind around that.

Nor could she stop feeling for a pulse and hoping she was wrong.

"Anything?" Titus asked, breathless from ten minutes of chest compression. He had been the first to search for a pulse. He had shouted for her to call 911 as he had begun CPR. So far, they hadn't been able to bring Hannah back, but Wren wasn't one to give up. Not on anyone or anything, and she wasn't willing to give up now.

"Nothing. I'll switch with you," she offered, knowing that one-armed chest compressions would be ineffective, but worried about Titus's ability to continue CPR.

"You've got one arm. You can't do chest compressions. Continue rescue breathing. It's possible she hasn't been here long." He began chest compressions again, his brow beaded with sweat, and he attempted to give Hannah a chance.

She had been warm when they'd found her, her body still soft with the potential for life, but the longer time went on without a heartbeat, the less likely it was she could be brought back.

Still, Wren couldn't give up—not if there was a chance—and she knew Titus felt the same.

She checked Hannah's airway again, listening for the sound of sirens and praying a rescue squad would arrive soon. If Hannah had any chance at all, she needed to receive advanced life support.

Wren gave two quick breaths and backed off, waiting and counting with Titus as he continued compressions. Sweat rolled down his temple, and his breathing was rapid with exertion. The phone she had used to dial 911 lay on the floor nearby, the 911 operator saying something Wren couldn't make out. She breathed again. Two quick puffs of air that raised and lowered Hannah's chest.

"Please, God," she prayed as Titus began another thirty compressions. "Please save her."

"Check for a pulse again," he said.

She lifted Hannah's wrist and thought she felt a tiny flutter of movement.

"I may have one," she said, her heart thrumming, hope soaring. She did not want to watch a woman she had always respected and admired die.

"Let's keep at it." He began chest compressions again, the faint sound of an ambulance filling the house. "Is the front door still unlocked?" he asked.

"I think so, but I'll double-check." She raced to the door and swung it open, allowing cold air to waft into the house.

Something fluttered on the floor under an ornate table that stood against the wall. She grabbed the small piece of paper and shoved it into her pocket before she ran back to help Titus again.

He was already giving rescue breaths.

"She's strong enough to make it," she said, hoping it was the truth.

"She is," he agreed, his eyes focused on Hannah. "Come on, Hannah. You have a family that needs you."

Paramedics rushed into the house, crowding into the room with equipment and a backboard.

Wren moved back, giving them space as Titus filled them in.

"So you don't know what happened to her?" one of the EMTs said.

"She was here when we arrived," Titus responded. "No sign of injury."

"Heart attack maybe," another EMT said. "She's at that age where women tend to miss the signs. Let's run an EKG, see if we get a shockable rhythm."

"Are you okay?" Titus asked, touching Wren's arm and looking into her eyes.

"I'm not the one who just performed twenty minutes of CPR. Are *you* okay?"

"Yeah, but I'll be better once I know Hannah is going to survive. What hospital are you taking her to?" Titus asked.

"We're going to Waldo County General. It's a level two trauma center."

"Are you airlifting her?" he asked.

"If there is a chopper available. If not, we'll drive." He turned back to the men and women gathered around Hannah and went to work stabilizing her.

"She's alive. That's encouraging," Wren said, her heart still pounding frantically. Two deputies down in two days? It seemed a stretch to think it was a coincidence.

"If we hadn't found her, the story might be a different one," Titus said grimly. He took her arm, encouraging her to walk outside with him. A few curious onlookers had gathered, most of them holding phones to their ears. Obviously, news was spreading.

"Wren!" An elderly woman in bright pink sweats and purple running shoes rushed toward her. Bette Sullivan had been Wren's high school physical education teacher. "Is it true that Hannah Simmons is dead?"

"Who told you that?" Wren asked. She hadn't spoken to anyone, and the only person Titus had spoken to was the 911 officer.

"That nosy Ella Faber peeked in the window when we heard that an ambulance was being dispatched."

"Heard from who?"

"I have no idea. Half the people here have police scanners. Even a fancy retirement community like this doesn't offer enough to keep active adults occupied." She shook her head, her hand settling on her narrow hips. "I've been tempted to throw in the towel, you know?"

"Throw in the towel how, Ms. Sullivan?"

"It's Mrs. Reginald now. I married Stan

Reginald three years ago. He died last week." She blinked rapidly, apparently trying to keep tears from flowing. "May God rest his wonderful soul."

"I'm so sorry for your loss, Mrs. Reginald."

"So am I. We had finally found each other. All those years of looking for Mr. Right at the grocery store and in church, and I find him in a community of old people that I never intended to live in."

"You didn't?" Wren asked, intrigued by the comment. Bette was the kind of person she would have expected to live in her cute little bungalow on Main Street for as long as she had breath in her lungs.

"Absolutely not! I was planning to live in my house until my nieces and nephews dragged me away and put me in a home, and then I was in that hit-and-run accident in the parking lot at Wegman's grocery store."

"Hit-and-run?" Wren asked, imagining the kind of damage that could be done to anyone hit by a vehicle. For an elderly person, that could be compounded by frail bones and the inability to heal quickly.

"Guy in a little white sports car backed right into me while I was walking across the lot. I fell and broke my arm." She lifted her left hand. "And a couple of ribs. Had to have surgery on the arm. I've got a metal plate and some screws in there now."

"Did they ever find the guy who hit you?" Titus asked.

"No. It was the craziest thing. The car was stolen. Why anyone would steal a vehicle and then sit in a crowded parking lot on a Saturday morning, I don't know." She shook her head. "I was upset about it. I do like to stay physically active, but while I was in rehab one day Lester came to visit. We know each other from church. He was concerned about my ability to care for myself once I left rehab, and he told me all about this wonderful place. Brought me a brochure and everything. Next thing I knew, I was agreeing to move here."

"Have you been happy with the choice?" Wren asked.

"That's an interesting question. Would I rather have my house and view of the cove? The yard I spent years planting and tending flower gardens in? The sunroom where all my nieces and nephews used to play after school? Probably. But when I moved here, I met Stan, and that is something I wouldn't have wanted to miss out on. If his heart hadn't given out, we'd be celebrating our fourth wedding anniversary soon."

"His funeral was last week?" Titus asked.

Bette nodded. "Yes. Lester thought it would be more practical for me to cremate the remains since I'm planning to move to Florida. He thought I might like to take Stan with me." She snorted. "Stan is in heaven. I'm sure that's much more pleasant than Florida."

"Was Stan hoping to go to Florida with you?" Wren asked, curious about the move and wondering if it had something to with the brochure she had seen.

"Oh. Yes. We invested in the project a year ago, and the more we looked at the brochure, the more convinced we were that we would be happier there than here. Not that the Maine coast isn't a lovely place, but it's cold and dreary half the year. At my age, I crave sunshine and warmth."

"That's perfectly understandable," Wren said, her pulse racing, the hair on the back of her neck standing on end. She knew this feeling. It was the one she got every time she was about to break a case. "So you paid into the investment company that owns the land in Florida?"

"Absolutely. According to Lester, it was a sure thing. We invest a certain amount, and as the units begin selling, we get our investment back plus two percent of the sale of every unit. We're talking more than a hundred units in a very sought-after area. They're selling in excess of three hundred thousand dollars. That's six hundred thousand for each investor."

"Then how does the sponsoring company make money?"

"They're very particular about who they allow to invest, and they only bring on ten investors for each project. Stan and I were fortunate enough to be included. We had to give cash, of course."

"Cash?" Wren was appalled by the thought. In her experience, cash deals were illegal deals.

"Well, yes. The money goes directly toward funding the project, and cash saves the company time."

Wren didn't point out that most monetary transactions were now done online, and she didn't ask any further questions. There was a moneymaking scheme going on at Sunrise Acres. Figuring out what kind of scheme and who was running it might lead her to Ryan's killer. Or, at least, to the reason for his death.

"You said Lester invited you to invest?" she asked, and Bette nodded.

"He approached Stan, but yes. It was Lester. Although we weren't supposed to tell anyone that." She lowered her voice to a whisper. "Lester said too many people would be trying to get in on the scheme, and he didn't have the time to deal with that. Not while he was running Sunrise Acres. I'd appreciate it if you didn't tell him I was the one who let the cat out of the bag."

"I won't, Mrs. Reginald."

"Call me, Bette. Everyone else does. Except Stan. Stan called me 'honey.'" Her voice broke. "I loved that. Now that he is gone, there'll be no one to call me that. I'll miss him when I move, but if there's a place in heaven for people to look down on this world, I know he'll smile when he sees me in Florida. Just the day before he died, he met with Lester and reminded him that we wanted property in exchange for our investment. Lester wasn't happy, but Stan said he would have to agree. Otherwise, we were going over his head."

"Did you have contact information for his immediate supervisor?" Wren asked.

"Stan might have. I'll look through his things. If I find something, do you want me to let you know?"

"I would appreciate it if you did." Wren handed her a business card.

"Thank you. By the way, you never did tell me, dear. Was it Hannah in the house?" She glanced at the house, her eyes wide with curiosity.

"Yes, but she isn't dead." Wren prayed that would continue to be the case.

"Was she shot? Like Ryan?"

"I can't answer any more of your questions, Bette. I'm sure the sheriff will keep everyone informed."

"Speaking of the sheriff," Titus said, his hand on Wren's shoulder as he steered her through the growing crowd. "Do you think someone has called him?"

"I'm sure he's heard." She watched the EMTs roll a stretcher outside. "They're transporting her."

"And you want to head to the hospital?"

"Yes, but first I'd like to talk to Lester about that investment deal he's offering people."

"I think that's a great idea," he agreed, his hand sliding from her arm to her hand. When his fingers curved through hers, when they were walking shoulder to shoulder, palm against palm, she didn't tell him that they were making a mistake. She didn't pull away or try to put distance between them.

She knew she would regret it.

She knew that he would probably break her heart again, but right then, with the sound of the gawking crowd and scream-ing ambulance echoing in her ears, and her mind spinning back to that long-ago day when her mother had been brutally

murdered and she had nearly died, Titus
felt like a safe place to be.

Titus's arms were shaking with adrenaline and fatigue, his heart racing in the
aftermath of what had happened. Wren
must have noticed, for she squeezed his
hand gently.

"Are you okay?" she asked. "You're
shaking."

"Just my arms. CPR for that amount of
time is brutal."

"I wish I could have helped."

"You did."

"Not much. Do you think she had a
heart attack?"

"I don't know. Maybe."

"Or? There were no marks on her that
I could see. No head injury. No blood."

"Stan had a heart attack."

"Bette's husband?" she asked, and he
nodded.

"I spoke to a lot of people who live here.
Most of them mentioned him. He was a

great guy. Hardworking. Used to be a real estate broker, so plenty of business savvy. He was also in really good shape. He played tennis every morning. Ran a half marathon a few months ago."

"Those things don't preclude heart disease," she said.

"They don't, but what is the likelihood that two seemingly healthy people would have heart attacks a week apart in this retirement village?"

"I…don't know."

"And what are the chances that those heart attacks aren't somehow related to Ryan's death?"

"That's another good question." She smoothed her hair, her dark eyes staring straight into his. "The fact that investment money had to be delivered in cash is troubling. The fact that Stan died the day after he told Lester he was going to go over his head—"

"We don't know that he did," Titus said.

"Bette said he told *her* that, but we have no idea what he said to Lester."

"No, but we can ask."

"And hope he tells the truth?" he said as they reached the clubhouse.

"And hope I can use whatever he tells me to find the truth for myself."

"Good plan. Your friends aren't around," he noted. The parking spot they'd been in was empty, his truck sitting nearly alone in the lot.

"Annalise had the phone conference. I told them to go ahead back to the farmhouse."

"You want to call them and let them know what's going on?"

"I want to speak with Lester. Everything else can happen later."

They walked into the building hand in hand, bypassing Alison's now-empty desk and heading down the hall toward Lester's office.

"Think he'll be in?" Wren asked as they approached the closed door.

"If I were him, and I knew what was going down at the old house, I'd be making a run for it, hoping to stay a step ahead of the police and any questions they might want to ask me."

"That's what I'd be doing. Let's see if Lester's mind works the same way." She knocked. When Lester didn't answer, she turned the doorknob.

The door swung open, revealing the office and the empty desk.

"He's gone." She strode across the room. "No convenient confession note lying on the desk."

"He doesn't strike me as a stupid man, and I doubt he'd leave proof of his crimes behind."

"Assuming he has committed crimes, he's left evidence. Everyone does."

"Well, it's up to the local police to find it," Titus pointed out.

"If he was scamming people out of money across state lines, it might be FBI jurisdiction. We'll have to see what the evidence shows, but for right now, you're correct. The sheriff and his department should handle it." There was a slight edge to her voice, and he pulled her toward him when she started walking back into the hall.

"You're not happy about letting the sheriff handle this?"

"One of his officers is dead. Another is near death. That seems like an awfully strange coincidence, and since I've never believed in coincidences, I'm leaning toward Ryan and Hannah knowing something that put them in the crosshairs of a killer."

"Hannah is the one who sent me to look at the house. It's strange that she was there. She said she didn't want to get involved because the sheriff asked her not to. She also said something about Abby's accident." He hadn't told Wren about the fact that Abby had at first claimed she'd been pushed down the stairs. He had wanted to gather more evidence, speak to some of the first responders and some of Abby's friends to see if their stories were the same. Stirring a pot that wasn't getting ready to boil over made no sense.

But, with Hannah being transported to the hospital and the possibility of whatever had happened to her being foul play, it was important to follow every potential lead.

"What?" Wren stepped into the hall, and he followed. The corridor was silent, bright light reflecting on the tile floor. There were photographs of residents lining the walls, happy pictures of good times being had at the village. Photographic evidence that Sunrise Acres was the place to be. A pretty facade hiding something dark and ugly? He was beginning to think so.

"Hannah said that Abby claimed to have been pushed."

Wren frowned. "I remember the doctor telling me that. He said she had sustained a head injury and was confused at first, but that she had changed her story. I asked Abby, and she confirmed that."

"What if she wasn't confused?"

"You're talking about attempted murder?" Her expression hardened.

"I don't know. I hadn't thought much about it until I heard Bette's story."

"About the hit-and-run?"

"Yes. That's two independent strong older women who have been unexpectedly injured and then visited by Lester while they're recovering."

"You don't think…" She shook her head, her dark eyes gleaming, her skin pale in the bright overhead light. "That's almost too much of a stretch to contemplate."

"Yet not so far-fetched it couldn't be true. I'd like to know how many other residents were in accidents prior to selling and moving here."

"If there were that many, don't you think there'd be rumors circulating around town? People notice things like that. At least, people in Hidden Cove would."

"Hannah was suspicious. That's why she asked me to come out here. She thought something was off. She couldn't put her finger on it."

"How long has this place been open?"

"Six years?"

"And how much suspicion does it raise when an elderly person is injured in an accident or a fall?" Wren continued.

"Not much."

"I'm going to have Radley do some digging around. He may be able to access local newspaper articles about accidents and contact the people who were in them. The *Hidden Cove Times* doesn't have a lot of news to post, so something like a hit-and-run or an accident like Abby's would probably make the paper." She pulled out her phone and dialed the number. They were walking through the corridor again, heading back to the lobby.

A woman's scream rent the air, the terror in her voice making Titus's blood run cold. He and Wren sprinted down the hallway, bursting out into the lobby at nearly the same time.

Alison was standing behind her desk, screaming hysterically as Lester Thomas tried to drag her away. He had an arm around her waist and a gun to her head, his eyes glittering with fear or madness.

"No one do anything stupid," he barked, the gun shaking as he pointed it at Wren and then at Titus.

"Stupid is trying to kidnap a woman in broad daylight with an FBI agent nearby," Wren responded, taking a step in his direction.

"Don't try to be a hero, Wren. It's not a good day for that." He released the safety on the gun and shoved the barrel against Alison's cheek. She stopped screaming and went still, her face devoid of color, her eyes wide with fear.

"You don't want to do this, Lester," Alison said. "We're not just coworkers, we're friends. I've never done anything to hurt you, and I never would." Her voice shook and the gun eased away from her cheek.

"Of course, I don't want to do this. I was

never in this to hurt anyone. I just wanted money to start a new life somewhere. This kind of stuff—" he waved the gun toward the hallway leading to his posh office "—gets old quickly. Listening to people complain because the flowers in the garden are pink instead of yellow. Listening to constant griping about the cafeteria food selections or the crack in the sidewalk out near the golf course? I could live the rest of my life never hearing another old person complain about stuff like that, and I'd be very happy doing it. But, things got out of hand, and people *have* been hurt. Let's not compound that."

"Let her go, Lester," Wren demanded. "You can leave. We're not going to stop you, but taking a hostage makes whatever you've done a federal offense."

"I'm not going to hurt her. I just don't want anyone trying to stop me." He edged toward the door, the gun pressed to Alison's side. "Stay in here. I'll drop her off outside of town. Once I'm sure no one is following."

Maybe he would.

Or maybe he would kill her.

Titus wasn't planning to take that chance. He met Wren's eyes. She shook her head. Just a subtle movement that he caught and understood. She wanted him to stand down.

I'll handle this, she mouthed as Lester walked outside, Alison moving stiffly beside him.

He thought she could. Easily. If she was armed. If she had two good hands. If she wasn't constrained by her badge and her sense of responsibility to protocol and procedure. He had no such compunctions. He had left law enforcement years ago. He was just a civilian watching a crime go down and planning to stop it.

He had his gun, but he didn't pull it.

No sense giving Lester advance warning.

Titus walked outside, an early-spring breeze tickling his cheeks as he followed

Lester across the parking lot. Although there was moisture in the air, hinting at another storm, the sun was still bright and high, blazing down onto the lot where Titus had parked the truck.

"I told you two to stay where you were!" Lester shouted, the gun dropping as he reached a shiny Cadillac and opened the door.

He was trying to shove Alison into the vehicle.

She wanted nothing to do with it and was struggling.

This was the opportunity Titus had been waiting for. He glanced at Wren one more time, and she shook her head again.

"Don't," she said, but he sprinted forward, tackling Lester and driving them both to the ground.

TEN

The sound of gunfire made the hair on Wren's arms stand on end. A bullet pinged off the pavement a few feet from the glossy black Cadillac as she raced after Titus, the reverberation mixing with the piercing sound of Alison's screams.

Wren grabbed Alison's arm, yanking her away from the struggling pair on the ground. Titus and Lester were fighting for control of the gun, and another shot could easily be fired.

"Run!" she shouted, giving the other woman a shove toward the building. "Call the police!"

"I already pushed the panic button under my desk," Alison cried, tears streaming down her face as she sprinted back to the clubhouse.

Wren turned her attention to Titus and Lester. It was an uneven match, Titus having the upper hand.

She tossed herself into the fray regardless, the way she had always done when it came to having her best friend's back.

Sirens were screaming again.

She ignored them. Titus had Lester's gun hand pressed against the pavement, held away from both of their bodies. Lester refused to let go of the gun.

She stepped on his wrist, applying just enough pressure for him to feel it.

"What are you doing?" he cried, going completely still, all the fight seeming to drain out of him.

"Let go of the gun," she commanded.

"I don't think so." He tried to twist his hand so that the barrel of the gun was pointed at her. She applied a little more pressure.

"I don't want to break your wrist, Lester.

I know for a fact that it's not fun to have only one functional hand. But I'll do it if I need to. Let go of the gun."

His fingers finally opened, and the gun slid to the pavement, the safety still off. She picked it up carefully, reengaged the safety and unloaded the firearm, then set it and the ammunition on the ground.

"Do you have any other weapons on you?" she asked, nearly shouting to be heard above the roar of approaching emergency vehicles.

"No," he replied.

"How about we check to make certain?" Titus yanked him to his feet.

"I'll frisk him," Wren offered. "It's going to be part of the crime report eventually. Might as well be an officer of the law who performs the task."

He nodded his agreement and stepped back, his gaze shooting toward the two police cruisers that had pulled into the parking lot. "Looks like the cavalry has arrived," he said.

"Good. We'll pass Lester off to them and head over to the hospital. I want to check on Hannah."

She frisked Lester one-handed, running her hand along his sides and up and down his legs. She patted his jacket pockets, pulling out a pocketknife and setting it on the ground next to the unloaded gun.

"I thought you didn't have any other weapons," she growled, using the voice she reserved for the dangerous felons she arrested. She wasn't sure how dangerous Lester was, but he was neck-deep in whatever was going on at Sunrise Acres. She felt confident he was connected to Ryan's murder.

"That's a utility knife," he snapped back. "I'd hardly call it a weapon."

"I would."

"So would I," Titus agreed. "Do you have anything else that might be construed as a weapon on you?"

"No. That's all." His beady eyes darted from Wren to Titus and back again.

"Everything okay over there?" one of the deputies called.

From a distance it looked like Levi—hair hidden beneath a uniform hat, compact muscular body moving with short, confident strides.

"I think we've got things under control," she said.

Lester tried to use the moment of distraction to his advantage. He whirled around, shoving her backward into Titus, and raced away, not even bothering to grab the gun as he ran past.

"Freeze!" Levi yelled, the force of his voice ringing through the silent parking lot. There were no gawkers here. No elderly people watching from a distance. They were all busy at the house by the pond, discussing the fact that Hannah had been found there, or they had taken shelter inside.

Lester continued to run, and she sprinted after him, Titus beside her. They were closing in. Just feet away from him. Almost close enough to tackle. Another foot, and she would bring him down.

A gunshot rang out, and Lester fell, his arms flailing, blood spurting from a wound in his back. A kill-shot that she was sure had hit his heart.

He landed on the blacktop, facedown, blood pooling beneath his body. She flipped him over, ignoring the pain in her broken wrist as she attempted to render aid and stanch the flow of blood.

"Use this." Titus handed her his jacket, and she pressed it against the wound. Lester's eyes were closed. If he was breathing, she couldn't feel it.

"Can you check for a pulse?" she asked, pressing harder as blood seeped through the jacket and bubbled around her hands, staining the white cast on her wrist pale pink. He was losing blood too quickly, all her efforts doing little to stanch the flow.

"Come on, Lester," she muttered. "Don't quit on us."

"No pulse," Titus said, adding his hands

to hers, pushing harder on the gushing wound.

She tried to focus on that, tried not to let her mind wander back to the night Ryan had pulled her over, to the way he had looked lying on the ground, blood seeping from his chest wound. She tried not to think about how little time she'd had to try to save him before the faux deputies had arrived and arrested her.

"Is he dead?" Levi asked as he reached them. He had tucked his firearm back into its holster and was barking into his radio, asking for backup and an ambulance.

"He's not breathing. No pulse," Titus replied.

"That's not what I wanted to hear," he muttered, crouching beside them and probing Lester's neck, searching for the jugular pulse.

"What were you thinking, Levi?" The sheriff jogged toward them, his black boots squeaking, his hat missing. He wore no tie. No jacket. Just a white shirt and black uniform pants. "He wasn't armed."

"He was." Levi pointed to the gun lying near Lester's vehicle.

"Not when you shot him." For once, Camden sounded tired rather than gruff, his red-rimmed eyes and five-o'clock shadow speaking of sleepless nights. "You're going to have to hand over your firearm." He held out his hand, waiting impatiently while Levi pulled it from its holster.

"When will I get it back?" he asked, still crouched near Lester's body, watching as blood stained the pavement beneath him.

"After Internal Affairs looks into this mess. For now, you're on administrative leave. Go back to the office. Fill out a report on what happened here. Turn in your badge. I'll speak to you when I return."

"The guy held a woman at gunpoint. I did what was necessary to keep him from hurting someone else." Levi attempted to defend his actions, but the sheriff held up a hand.

"We'll discuss it later. When we don't have an FBI agent sitting beside us."

"I've got nothing to hide."

"You should probably do what the sheriff suggests," Wren said, her body humming with adrenaline, her mind buzzing with thoughts that bounced in one direction and then another.

Lester had been scamming elderly people out of their hard-earned money. She didn't think he had been working alone. If he died, there would be no interrogation, no offer of a plea deal in exchange for information.

An ambulance arrived, and the crew swept in, continuing the fight to save Lester's life. She didn't like giving up on anyone, but she didn't think he was going to make it. "It's too bad," she murmured, accepting antiseptic wipes from an EMT who suggested she wipe the blood from her hands.

"Lester's death?" Titus asked, his teal-blue eyes focused on Lester's pale, prone body.

"If he dies, yes. It's a waste of a life, and…" She glanced at the body, feeling bad for what she was thinking.

"And the possibility of getting any information out of him?" Titus asked.

"Yes. I feel guilty thinking about that when the guy may not survive."

"Don't," the sheriff cut in. "Anyone in law enforcement would be thinking the same. I need to get both your statements." His gaze dropped to Wren's bloodstained cast. "Do you want to get changed and then meet me at my office? I'll finish up here, and then we can go over what happened."

All his arrogance and aggression seemed to have disappeared. Maybe losing Ryan and potentially losing Hannah had sobered him.

"How is Hannah?" Titus asked, and the sheriff shook his head.

"I haven't been to the hospital yet. I was

on my way there when this call came in. From what the doctors are saying, she's clinging to life."

"Do they think it was a heart attack?"

"They don't know. I told her to stay away from this place. I wish she had listened." He shook his head, ran a hand over his dark hair.

"Why did you tell her that?" Wren asked, curious. Had he suspected something was going on? Or had he been part of it?

"Because my office doesn't need a bad reputation, and she seemed fixated on the condition of the old house she was found in. I was worried she would stir up trouble with the people who live here and the company that owns the property."

"Garner Investment Initiative?" Titus asked, and Camden nodded.

"Yes. They're bigwigs in the investment property world. I wasn't too keen when they showed up and said they wanted to buy this piece of land and develop it, but the town voted to allow it, and I'm not one to dwell on my losses."

"Plus, the people in town seem happy with Sunrise Acres," Wren said, fishing for more information and hoping he would provide it.

"Yes, they are. Which is another reason I didn't want to stir up trouble. If the people of this town are happy, I'm happy. Although, right now, I wouldn't call my feelings anything close to that. Now, if you two don't mind, I need to process this scene so I can get back to the office, write up the reports and contact the state police to begin the internal investigation into the shooting." He watched the EMTs working on Lester. "I'm hoping he survives, but I have a bad feeling about this. Come in when you're ready. If I'm not there, you can meet me at the county hospital. I want to check in and see how Hannah is doing."

He walked away without another word, his shoulders slumped, his posture speaking of fatigue and defeat.

"It's been a rough few days for the sheriff's department," she said, more to her herself than to Titus.

"Yes. It has. You know what I'm thinking that means?"

"That someone in the sheriff's department was involved in this scheme?"

"Maybe more than one person."

"That Ryan was involved?" she added, allowing herself to voice a thought she would rather not have entertained.

However, the fact was that she was an officer of the law.

Her job was to see justice done.

No matter who the perpetrator was.

"Honestly? I think he was either involved or knew about it. His death might have been a hit designed to keep him from going to the authorities. Or maybe he got greedy and started asking for more than what he was already receiving."

"Knowing Ryan, either is possible. He had a good heart, but he always liked to skirt the law." Tears burned her eyes, but she didn't let them fall. Not this time. She had too much to do, too many questions to ask. She didn't have time to mourn. She didn't have time for self-care or processing.

She wanted answers, and she intended to find them.

"I remember that about him," Titus said, the sympathy in his voice and his gaze making her heart ache. She wanted to step into his arms and feel the warmth of his body pressed against hers. She wanted to lay her head against his chest and listen to his heart beat its slow and soothing rhythm.

But she had work to do, answers to find. Even if she didn't, she would probably be too scared of having her heart broken to allow herself to be comforted by Titus. Wouldn't she?

Maybe it was time to change that.

Maybe it was time to take chances and allow herself to be open to possibilities. No relationship was without its trials and its hurts, but some relationships weathered the storms and became stronger because of them.

What if she could have that with Titus? The strengthening bond, the growing closer every year, the sharing of dreams and hopes, fears and hurts?

She headed across the parking lot, her chest heavy with regret and sorrow and longing for things she couldn't have. Ryan back. Lester alive. Hannah healthy.

Titus in her life once again.

He opened the truck door and she climbed into the cab, pulling the seat belt across her lap and waiting as he rounded the vehicle.

It felt right being in the truck with him, heading back to the farmhouse where they had spent so much of their youth. She had loved him then. She had loved him always. That love had changed during their friendship, morphing into something she hadn't expected and hadn't known what to do with.

She was older and hopefully wiser.

If she had the opportunity again, she would tell him how she felt. She would let him know that her feelings had changed, and she would see where that brought them.

"You're quiet," he said as he pulled onto the road.

"Just thinking."

"Want to share?"

"It's nothing to do with the case," she hedged.

"That doesn't mean you can't share."

"I was wondering what would have happened if I had told you how I felt at prom."

He was silent for a moment, his jaw set and his focus on the road. Then he held out his hand. She took it, curving her fingers through his, studying his profile and wondering how she had gone so many years without contacting him.

"I would like to think that we would have made it," he finally said. "That I would have realized how deep my feelings for you were, and we would have gotten married and had our careers and kids and our lives. I'd like to think that we would have had our happily-ever-after."

"I never needed that," she said, but she had wanted it. Secretly. In the deepest part of her heart.

"No. You didn't," he replied. "You probably still don't."

With you, I do, she almost said, but the words stuck in her throat, and by the time she felt ready to speak them, they had reached the farmhouse and he was parking the truck.

They cleaned up first, scrubbing their hands and arms in the mudroom sink. Wren had changed into clean clothes and grabbed jeans and a shirt from the closet in the guest room where Abby had always kept clothes for foster kids or anyone else who needed them. She had handed the clothes to Titus, and he had changed quickly. The jeans were a little loose, but anything was better than the blood-spattered outfit he had been wearing. After he changed, he joined Wren in the living room. The smell of charred wood and now mildew had begun to permeate Abby's home. The sooner Titus began restoration, the better. Right now, though, he needed to focus on helping Wren find out the truth about what had happened to Ryan. The brochures he had kept in the attic connected him to both properties. Had he been aware of the investment scheme? Had he been part of it? Those were questions they needed to answer.

Annalise was still on a conference call. Radley was pacing the kitchen impatiently.

"What is going on in this town?" he asked as Wren and Titus entered the room. "I leave you for an hour, and you nearly get killed by some guy who runs a retirement village? That's not cool, Wren."

"I wasn't nearly killed."

"That's not what Abby says."

"You spoke with Abby?"

"Of course I did. She called me when she couldn't reach you."

"She was trying to reach me?" Wren pulled out her phone out. "I guess she was. I had the volume turned off while we were touring."

"She heard through the grapevine that there was a gunman at Sunrise Acres. She also heard there was a body, and that you were somehow involved."

"If by 'involved' you mean I was there, then yes. It's true. I was involved." She poured two cups of coffee and handed one to Titus.

"I'm assuming you plan to explain that?"

"I do, but Titus and I need to drive to the county hospital. Remember Deputy Simmons?"

"Hannah? Sure."

"We found her in the old house out on Sunrise Acres. She was in bad shape." She explained the rest quickly, then handed him the piece of paper she'd found. "Since

I know you hate hospitals, I'd like you to head to this address and see if there's anything interesting there."

"By interesting, you mean anything to do with investment schemes or Ryan's death?"

"I mean anything that seems out of the ordinary. I'm not sure the note is connected to what happened to Ryan or Hannah, but I can't rule it out until I know what's there. Can you also check the local papers and see if you can find anything about accidents involving the elderly?"

"Out at Sunrise Acres?"

"There or anywhere in town. I'm curious to see if there is a connection between accidental deaths and Sunrise Acres."

"I'm on it." He walked from the room, and Wren turned her attention to Titus. "Do you want to go with him or come with me?"

"We've always been a good team. I don't see any reason to mess with that dynamic."

She smiled wearily, her eyes never leaving his face. She was studying him as if she was memorizing his features and putting his picture away somewhere deep in her mind.

"What's wrong?" he asked.

"Nothing. I just…" She shook her head. "Just a feeling I have that we're going to uncover things that someone would prefer remain hidden. That could be dangerous, and I don't want anything to happen to you."

"I can take care of myself, Wren. You know that."

"I'd have said the same about Ryan, and look what happened." She took a sip of coffee and set the mug in the sink. "I've had way too much of this stuff lately. Let's get out of here. The drive is going to take a while, and I'm hoping by the time we arrive, Hannah will be conscious and able to speak."

"And if she isn't?"

"I want to know who visits her. The sheriff seemed awfully eager." She grabbed a wool coat from the hall closet and slid into it.

"They've been working together for years. It's only natural that he would want to be updated on her condition."

"I know, but the guys who handcuffed me were dressed in Hidden Cove deputy uniforms. The sheriff tried to argue that they were knockoffs patched together by men who were trying to trick me, but I know what I saw. They were in uniform. Where do you think they got those?"

"A uniform supply store?"

"They'd have had to order it online. There isn't one around here. And the pants, shirt and jackets aren't cheap. I can't imagine two low-life criminals having the funds for that."

"That doesn't rule out the possibility," he reminded her.

"True, but I think they were given those uniforms by someone who had access to them."

"The sheriff?"

"It makes sense. He has access to everything. It's a small force. He issues the uniforms and keeps track of what needs to be ordered. He could even have provided the vehicle."

"Because he needed to get rid of Ryan? Then why have the perps shoot him while you were there? Why not wait until he was alone and there were no witnesses?"

"Those are good questions. I've been trying to come up with reasonable answers. Ryan wanted to tell me something that night. He pulled me over purposely. I thought it was a joke, and I was trying to give him a hard time about wasting town resources, but he was serious. Probably more serious than I've ever seen him. He said we needed to talk, and it needed to be in a place where no one from town could see us. He told me he was in trouble, and that he needed my help. It seemed bizarre at the time, and it still does." She dug through the closet again and pulled out another wool coat. "This was Ryan's. He wasn't as tall as you, but he was broader. Put it on so you don't freeze."

"I'm not going to freeze," he said, shrugging into the coat anyway, his heart broken for Wren and Abby's loss. "Did Ryan have a chance to say anything to you after you got out of your vehicle?"

"Just what I told you. That he was in trouble, and that he needed my help." She frowned. "Actually, he said he had something for me. I'd forgotten that until just now."

"What was it?"

"I have no idea. He was shot before he had a chance to give it to me."

"He was in his cruiser, right?"

"Yes."

"Did anyone check that?"

"I'm sure the sheriff's department did. We can ask if anything was found. If I'd remembered, I would have already done that."

"It was a traumatic night. It isn't surprising that your memories of it aren't clear. How about I ask the sheriff after I check out the address you gave me?" Radley suggested as he stepped back into the room. He had changed into a dark suit and white shirt, and he looked exactly like the federal law enforcement officer Titus knew him to be.

"You're going to ask to be allowed to see the cruiser?" she responded.

"Why not? If he says no, maybe I can at least get a list of what they found inside it."

"All right. Give it a shot, but be careful. I have no idea what side of this the sheriff is standing on."

"I will be." He walked outside, and Titus offered Wren his hand.

"We should get going, too," he said.

She hesitated and then placed her hand in his. "Yes. I guess we should," she said.

They walked outside together, the farm stretching out in every direction, sunlight gleaming in emerald grass and yellowed cornstalks. The day was beautiful and bright, but there were clouds on the horizon. A storm was blowing in. Titus hoped it would hold off until they reached the hospital. This time of year, roads could get icy and travel could be difficult.

He wanted to reach the hospital and make certain Hannah was doing okay. And then he wanted to head to the sheriff's office. They needed answers, and they needed them quickly. Something dangerous and deadly was happening in Hidden Cove, and the sooner they figured out what it was, the sooner they could stop it.

ELEVEN

Hannah's condition had stabilized, but she was on life support, machines pumping oxygen into her lungs and an IV catheter forcing fluid into her body. Only two people were allowed in her room at one time. Hannah's family had been on vacation in Cape Cod. Her children and husband were on the way but wouldn't arrive for another few hours.

Until then, her police comrades were standing in for them.

At least, that's what Levi had said when Wren had entered the room and found him there. Titus was out in the hall, waiting for his turn to visit Hannah. Wren had asked if Levi was already finished with his report, and he had responded with a curt nod and a quick affirmative. They had spent the last few minutes awkwardly avoiding conversation about what had happened at Sunrise Acres. If she had been there in an official capacity, she would have asked every question that she wanted to, and she would have demanded answers.

Instead, she was there out of concern and in the unfounded hope that Hannah might be able to tell her what had happened.

"She doesn't look good." Levi finally broke the silence. "Her family is going to be devastated when they hear that she overdosed."

"Overdosed?" That was the first Wren had heard of it, and the news took her by surprise.

"That's what the doctors think. She had high levels of cocaine in her system. And they found this." He turned Hannah's lax arm over to reveal a pinprick and bruise on the skin of her inner elbow.

"There aren't track marks," Wren said,

dismissing the idea that Hannah had been a secret addict. She had seen plenty of men and woman who were users who had rows of needle marks on their arms and abdomens and thighs.

"Maybe it was her first time. I'd like to think so," he said, the mournful tone of his voice belying the quickness and willingness of his reply. He had no problem believing that Hannah had shot herself up with cocaine. That bothered Wren. She always went to bat for her coworkers. She always believed in them. She always trusted that they were what they portrayed themselves to be—upright and honest men and women.

Otherwise, she couldn't trust them enough to work together on cases that often required life-risking moments.

"Did they find anything else in her system?" she asked, making sure her tone was even and calm. People responded to tragedies in different ways. Perhaps believing Hannah had injured herself was easier for Levi than believing she had been the target of a violent crime.

"They did actually. A large amount of tramadol in her system. It's a prescription painkiller."

"I know what it is," she said. The narcotic was well-known to lead to addiction. "Does she suffer from chronic pain? Has she had surgery lately? She had to have gotten the prescription somewhere."

"Not that I know of. It's possible it's one of her husband's prescriptions. She's always been healthy as a horse. Jim has been sick for years. I'm sure he's had all kinds of painkillers."

"I see. You think she overdosed on tramadol and then went to the old house on Sunrise Acres and shot herself full of cocaine? For what purpose?" she asked, barely managing to keep the edge out of her voice. None of this was ringing true to her, and she couldn't begin to imagine why Levi was so willing to believe it.

"I'm wondering..." He rubbed the back of his neck and shrugged.

"What?"

"If she had something to do with Ryan's death. Maybe she was involved and couldn't deal with the guilt."

"So she attempted suicide?"

"That's what it seems like, don't you think? She didn't accidently consume that much pain medication, and she certainly didn't accidently get her hands on cocaine and shoot up with it."

Wren's phone rang, saving her from having to fake interest in Levi's theory. Hannah had been a fixture in the community for decades. She had served the town the best way she knew how, and she had given her all to a job that she had loved. Even after her husband's diagnosis, she had maintained her career with the sheriff's department. She deserved way more loyalty than what Levi was giving her.

"Hello?" Her voice was sharp, and this time she didn't care. As soon as she finished the conversation, she planned to give Levi a piece of her mind.

"Hey, it's me," Radley said. "Is everything okay? You sound tense."

"I'm fine."

"How is Hannah?"

"Stable but on life support. They think she OD'd. Cocaine and tramadol."

"That's a strange combination. Which did she consume first?"

"I'm not sure, but her levels of each were high enough to kill her." She glanced at Levi. He had crossed the room and was staring out the window into the parking lot below. They were on the second floor, a fire escape jutting up above the window frame. The sun had disappeared behind thick gray clouds. Snow clouds. Abby would love that. She had always been a big fan of cold weather and snow.

"Hmm. Interesting. Seems to me she may have had a little help overdosing."

"I was thinking the same," she responded, glancing at Levi again. She knew he was listening, and she thought about stepping into the hall, but she didn't want to leave Hannah.

"The question is who helped her and why?"

"I don't suppose you found anything at the address I gave you or got anything at the sheriff's office that will help us figure it out?" She expected him to say no, not anticipating that the sheriff had cooperated.

"The address was a dead end. It was a summer rental. Cute cottage. Windows boarded up for the season. Doors locked. If anyone was in there, they didn't open the door, and I didn't have a warrant to search the property."

"Was there any sign that Hannah had been there?" she asked.

"Tread marks in the gravel driveway that were left recently. They could have belonged to her marked car. According to Sheriff Wilson, they haven't been able to find it."

"You'd think it would have been parked at Sunrise Acres if she'd overdosed there." She stepped close to the door and lowered her voice, her gaze focused on Levi. He was doing his best to pretend he wasn't listening, but the tension in his shoulders and neck told her he was paying very close attention to what she was saying.

"Yeah. You would, but like I mentioned, I suspect she had help. Speaking of the sheriff, he let me go through the box of evidence that was collected at the scene of Ryan's murder and from his work vehicle. Do you have a piece of paper and a pen?" Radley asked.

Her heart jumped at the question, and she grabbed both from the nightstand near the bed. "Sure. What do you have?"

"There was a handwritten note. The sheriff wouldn't let me take photos of anything so I can't send you a picture, but I jotted down what it said. It's cryptic, but maybe if you can figure things out, we'll find Ryan's killer."

"I hope so. Ryan and Hannah deserve justice."

"And you and Abigail deserve closure," he said so kindly her eyes filled with tears she wasn't going to let fall.

"Our focus is on justice," she reminded him. "We find the bad guys, and we put them away."

"That's not your story when we're working cases for other families. You always say that closure is a key component to healing, and that if we can give the families of victims the truth, they can use it as a springboard to move forward."

She did say that. She had learned the value of truth and closure the hard way. She had watched her mother die. She had fought for her own life. She had survived and then spent months in the hospital and even longer waiting for the perpetrator— her mother's abusive second husband—to be tried and convicted of the crime.

It wasn't a story she shared, but it was a truth she had lived. She understood both sides of the law intimately, and she had always used that to help ease the pain of victims and their families.

"If you're done tossing my words back at me, how about you read me the note?" she said, and he chuckled.

"Sure. It says, 'I always keep my secrets in the same place. Remember finding them? Look there, and you'll find more, sis. I love you, R.'"

She wrote as he read, her hand shaking, her pulse racing. "It's signed by Ryan, and obviously meant for me. Why didn't the sheriff tell me about it before now?"

"He said that he didn't want you to interfere with the investigation. I'll say that I think he was feeling intimidated by having the Feds descend on his town. He wanted to maintain control of the case, and he wasn't willing to give you anything that might help your investigation."

"He should have hung his pride and ego at the door of his office and done the right thing," she growled. "Because I know exactly what that note means. Is Annalise still there?"

"Where else would she be?"

"I'm going to grab Titus and head back your way. If I'm right, whatever secrets Ryan had are hidden in our old hangout on the beach. Ryan wasn't supposed to know about it, but he followed us there one day. Totally ruined it for me, but I still went back a few times. He used to hide his cigarettes and beer there. I haven't thought about it in years."

"You want me to let the sheriff know?"

"I'll decide on my way. For right now, let's plan on doing this ourselves. If we find something that will help with the case, we'll hand it over to the local authorities. I'm heading out. ETA is an hour and twenty."

"See you when you get here."

She tucked the paper into her pocket and turned toward the door. "I'll be back later today. I'll update you on any developments then." She tossed the words over her shoulder as she reached for the door handle.

"That won't be necessary," Levi replied.

"What…" She turned, her voice trailing off as she saw the gun in his hand and the look in his eyes.

"We'll go find your brother's hiding place together. That will save me time and effort later."

"You don't really think I'm walking out of this hospital without screaming my head off and warning everyone in earshot that you have a gun, do you?" she said. He'd made his move too quickly, and she was going to use it to her advantage.

"Through the hospital? No, but that's not where we're headed."

He grabbed her arm, yanking her against his side, the barrel of the gun digging into the side of her face. "Let me tell you what's going to happen. We're climbing out the window and going down the fire escape. We're sticking this close the entire time, and if you give me any trouble while we're getting out, I'll shoot Hannah through the heart. You've seen what a good shot I am, so don't try to run or fight me. Even if you live, she'll die, and you know how her family will mourn since you and Abigail have had to live with the same kind of pain."

He smiled, the darkness in his eyes reminding her of the look she had seen in the eyes of serial killers she had interviewed. A veneer of emptiness layered over pure evil. He wasn't bluffing. If she didn't cooperate, he would kill Hannah.

"All right," she agreed, and his smile broadened.

"Ryan was right. You really are the smart one in the family. Maybe if he had gone to you sooner with his concerns, he would still be alive, and I would be in jail."

"For tricking people into investing their life savings in Lester's real estate scheme?"

"Lester's?" He shoved her toward the

window. "Maybe you're not as smart as you seem."

"So it was your idea?" she asked, trying to buy time, to give a nurse or a doctor or even Titus a chance to walk into the room and intervene.

"I know what you're doing," he responded, his voice ice-cold and hard. "You can continue trying to waste time hoping someone is going to walk into the room and save you or you can cooperate and help me get what I want."

"What do you want?" she asked.

"What your brother stole from me. I don't mind waiting and, to be honest, I don't mind killing. One of the reasons I joined the sheriff's department was to find out what it was like to shoot someone without having to go to jail for it. The next person who walks into this room will be dead before he takes three steps. Want to test that and see if I can pull it off?"

She went cold at his words, her body humming with fear. Anyone could walk in, and any loss of life would be inconceivably tragic. She couldn't stop picturing Titus lying in a pool of his own blood.

"Open the window and let's get out of here," she said, her voice as cold as his had been. She knew how to hide fear, and she knew how to use adrenaline as fuel for clarifying thoughts and solidifying plans. She couldn't fight him now, not when there were so many people nearby, but once they were outside, she should be able to take him down.

Be patient.

Abigail had spent years trying to teach Wren how to do that. The lessons had stuck with her, and she used the hard-won skill as Levi manhandled the lock into an open position and slid the window up.

"Let's go," he said, yanking her against his side again.

The fire escape had been upgraded at some point from an old-fashioned pull-down ladder to a narrow staircase drilled into the side of the brick building.

She thought about shoving Levi over the railing. She didn't care if she went with him, but there were people down below, wandering through the parking lot unaware that a killer was making his way toward them. If she failed, if he didn't go over the side, he might start taking potshots at strangers to punish her.

She needed to bide her time and wait for an opportunity.

The beach might offer that.

The hiding place Ryan was talking about was in a small cave on the beach at the end of the access road behind Abigail's property. Carved into a granite wall that overlooked the rocky sand and buffeted by wild waves that kept most people from spending time there, the cave had once been used by someone who had carved hand-and footholds into the face of the cliff. High enough to stay dry and low enough to be accessible, it had been the perfect place to spend hot summer days.

"Good job," Levi said as they reached

pavement and headed across the parking lot. There were a few people heading toward the hospital, distracted by their own troubles and apparently oblivious to Wren's.

"I knew you would cooperate," he said as they reached a black sedan. "But it's a long drive back to the cove and I don't trust you. So how about we do something to guarantee you don't cause me trouble."

He moved before the words registered, and she barely had time to react as he raised the gun and swung it down toward her temple.

She jerked sideways, and the blow hit the side of her face. She felt skin split and blood seeping from the wound on her cheek. He hit her again as she reeled from the first blow.

She saw stars and darkness, and then she saw nothing at all.

Titus glanced at his watch and paced the waiting room for what seemed like the hundredth time. The hospital had labeled the room a family lounge, but it looked like every other waiting room he had ever been in. Plastic couches and cheap side tables that were piled high with magazines. A bin of toys sat in one corner, and a television was hanging from the wall. He had been in the room for less than a half hour, and he was already sick of it.

He walked into the hall, tempted to walk past the nurses station. He had Hannah's room number. He didn't plan to enter the room. He just wanted a quick peek in to make certain that everything was okay.

To make certain *Wren* was okay.

He had sent a text ten minutes ago, and he had received no response. He had tried again five minutes later with the same result. It wasn't like her to ignore communication, and he was beginning to worry.

Beginning?

He was past worrying and moving toward action.

She was in a hospital, sitting with a deputy sheriff in a room that could easily be seen by anyone in the hall. He didn't know how anything horrible could have happened, but the knot of dread in his stomach was saying it was possible.

He walked past the nurses, offering a quick smile as he moved down the hall. His phone rang as he turned a corner that led to Hannah's room. He answered, thinking it was Wren, maybe with more information than she wanted to text.

"Hello?" he said.

"Titus. Radley Tumberg. I'm trying to reach Wren."

"Funny, so am I," he said, jogging to the room and stepping inside, his pulse racing with fear. Aside from Hannah, the room was empty, a cold breeze ruffling curtains and scattering a few pieces of paper across the floor.

"I called her a few minutes ago," Radley continued. "I had some information I wanted to share. She said the two of you would be heading my way, and that we'd meet at the farmhouse."

"I haven't seen or heard from her since she went into Hannah's room," Titus said, walking to the window and looking out. There was a fire escape that led to the ground. "This isn't good," he muttered.

"What?" Radley demanded, his voice harsh with concern.

"The window's open. I think they went out the fire escape."

"They?"

"Wren and Deputy Levi Goodwin."

"I met him the night Ryan's apartment was ransacked," he said. "You think they're together?"

"I don't see how they can't be. They were in the room together. Now they're both gone." He climbed out the window, pulled it closed behind him and then scrambled down the metal stairs. When he reached pavement, he saw the first drop of blood. There were several more nearby.

"Someone was bleeding," he muttered.

"What did you say to Wren? Why were we supposed to be heading back that way?"

"I found a note in the evidence box the sheriff had. It was from Ryan. For Wren. He said that she needed to look in the place where he used to hide his secrets. He had more secrets hidden there. I can grab it and read it to you if you think it will help."

"I know exactly what Ryan was talking about. There's a cave on the beach that we used to hang out in. It's carved into the cliff that overlooks the cove. He must have hidden something there."

"And Levi wants it," Radley muttered, his frustration obvious.

"If they're together—and I think they are—there has to be a reason she isn't answering her phone."

"He shot Lester Thomas today. The sheriff implied it wasn't justified," Radley said. "He was waiting for Levi to give a statement, but he hadn't shown up. I don't think the sheriff has any idea he was at the hospital. According to Wren, the doctors think Hannah overdosed, but based on what Wren told me, it seems unlikely."

"What did she say?"

"An overdose of tramadol mixed with an injection of cocaine. I think it's more likely someone tricked her into taking too much pain medication. When she didn't die from that, she was injected with the cocaine."

"You think Levi is responsible?" Titus asked, running to his truck and hopping in. If he was right—and he thought he was—Wren and Levi were on their way to the private beach near Abigail's place.

"Levi or Lester, or both. I'd say Levi is the ringleader. Lester doesn't seem smart enough to come up with a scheme that has probably netted them hundreds of thousands of dollars already."

"And, when Lester realized Hannah had been found and was alive, he tried to run. He probably has a stash of money somewhere that he planned to take on the road with him. Only his partner in crime shot him." Titus pulled onto the road, pressing the accelerator to the floorboard, his mind racing with possibilities.

"Ryan was probably involved. He may have wanted too much of the profit or he became remorseful and decided they needed to close the operation down, so he had to be killed."

"That makes sense, but there is another possibility," Titus said. "Remember Stan Reginald's death?"

"Yeah."

"He died right after he asked to be given a unit from the new retirement village rather than money from sales. Maybe the retirement village in Florida doesn't exist. Maybe it's just a bunch of pretty pictures designed to get vulnerable people to invest money they spent their lives earning. And maybe Stan kept pushing to get his way—"

"And was murdered because of it?" Radley cut in.

"He had a heart attack. Supposedly. But from what I've heard he was in good health. His widow told me Lester had tried to talk her into cremating the remains."

"She didn't?"

"No. Maybe you can have the coroner look at the case again. I'm on my way back to the farm. ETA forty-five minutes. Call the sheriff and let him know what's going on. We need a plan to access that cave without drawing attention to ourselves.

"Or we need to arrive before Wren and Levi," Radley suggested. "You know where it is, right?"

"Yes."

"I'm heading to the road on foot. They can't have made it back this soon. If you can get here before them, you can take me to the cave. We'll set up a surprise for Levi that he's not going to forget."

"How much of a head start do you think they have?" Titus asked as he sped along the highway.

"Ten minutes? Maybe a few more."

"I'm not sure I can pass them, but I'll try."

"Don't try too hard. If I know Wren, she's going to take him to the wrong beach before she takes him to the right one. There is no way she isn't going to buy time."

"I still need to be there early enough to get into the cave."

"*We* have to," Radley corrected.

"As long as Wren isn't hurt, I'm good with that."

"You're not the only one who cares about her, Titus. She's a great agent and a fantastic supervisor, and she's also a really good friend to all of us. There isn't one of us who wouldn't put his life on the line for her. Whatever it takes, we're getting her back safely." He disconnected before Titus could respond.

That was fine.

They understood each other. That was what mattered. Keeping Wren safe was their priority, and if that meant arriving at the beach before Levi and Wren, Titus had every intention of doing it.

The storm clouds that had been gathering suddenly opened, and sleet battered the truck's hood and windshield. Although the granite rock would be slippery and the climb treacherous, there was no way he wouldn't be in that cave when Wren and Levi arrived.

"Please, God. Keep her safe," he prayed as he took the exit and merged onto the road that led through town.

TWELVE

Wren woke with a splitting headache and someone shaking her hard enough to rattle her teeth. She would have opened her eyes, but they felt glued shut, her headache too painful for her to do more than fall back into the darkness she had been pulled out of.

She wanted to sink back into the velvety bliss of it, but her tormentor shook her again.

"Wake up, sunshine! Time to go!"

She recognized the voice but not the singsong quality of it. She managed to force her eyes open and look into Levi's face. For a moment, she had no idea why he was there, why he was shaking her or why her head hurt.

Then he pressed a gun beneath her chin and everything came flooding back.

"Here we are. At the beach," he growled, his face so close she could see the veins in his bloodshot eyes and the streaks of gray in his hair. "And it's sleeting, so the place is empty. Perfect for our purposes, don't you think?"

"Sure," she managed to say, her head swimming, her stomach rebelling. Still, an empty beach gave her the advantage. Even with a head injury and one hand, she had a chance at taking him down. She just had to time it right.

"Glad you're suddenly so agreeable. Let's go. I have a plane to catch this evening, and I don't have time to play around." He yanked her by her broken wrist, pulling her from the back seat of his car. Pain shot up her arm, but she didn't give him the pleasure of seeing her respond to it.

He was waiting, studying her face for some sign that he had hurt her. She gave him a second, the sleet that was falling in heavy sheets cooling her face and sharpening her focus.

"Thanks," she said with a smile that she knew would infuriate him. He raised the gun, and she thought he might backhand her with it. She knew his kind. She had lived with more than one of them when her mother was alive—bullies who thrived on intimidating and causing pain.

"If I didn't need you, I'd kill you right now, Wren," he spat, dragging her away from the car and toward the cove.

"You shouldn't have knocked me out before you knew for sure where we were going," she said, her mind so fuzzy she was afraid she might pass out again.

He stopped and swung around, his grip tight on her arm. She thought he might be bruising the bone. "What are you talking about?" he nearly shouted. "You said the cove, and that's where we are."

"I said the beach. I was talking about the one near Abby's place."

"You're lying," he roared, the gun

pressed to her forehead, his intention obvious. He wanted to pull the trigger, and he could do it. Easily.

"Why would we hang out here in the summer? It's crowded. There's no privacy. There certainly isn't anything here that hasn't already been discovered. If we'd had a hiding place, it would have been the same one as a dozen other kids," she said, keeping her voice cool and her gaze as direct as she could manage with her head spinning.

He cursed, shoving her away yet obviously believing her. "Back in the car. You try anything stupid, and I'll kill you, and then I'll kill Abby. And she won't die quickly. I'll make it as slow and as painful as possible."

He shoved her again, and she stumbled to the car, climbing in through the still-open back door. There was a small pool of blood on the seat, and she touched the split skin on her cheek. The blood had congealed. At least, she didn't have to worry about bleeding to death.

Yet.

"Keep your head down. You pop it up one time, and I'll shoot the first person I see." He climbed into the front and pulled off the beach, the car bouncing over rocks, and onto the parking lot.

She didn't dare raise her head to look around, but she knew the way to the beach access road. She knew how long it took to get there from town. She counted stop signs and stoplights, refusing to give in to temptation and jump from the car. If something happened and she was hurt or killed, there would be no one to protect Abby from Levi.

She patted her pockets, trying to find her phone, hoping to sneak in a call while he was driving.

He chuckled. "I know what you're doing," he said in the same voice he had used to wake her. Creepy and weird and a lot more frightening than she wanted to admit.

"Yeah. What?" She would play his games and let him think he was winning if that meant surviving.

"Looking for your phone, but I'm not stupid. As a matter of fact, I'm a member of Mensa. Did you know that?"

"Why would I?"

"You wouldn't. I've done my time here, pretending to be like everyone else, working a dull job with dull coworkers and thinking I might like to try something different one day. When my wife got sick, and I realized how little money I was making and how far in debt we were going to be after her treatment, I decided I wanted something better."

"So you decided to steal money from people who worked hard all their lives? People you have known since you were a kid? People who respect and trust you?"

"Sure. Why not?" he said casually, as

if stealing from people he had known all his life meant nothing to him.

"And you're leaving tonight? Taking your family...where?"

"Family? Sorry. I have better things to do with my time than take care of a woman who is still complaining about being sick two years after she finished cancer treatment. And the kids are leeches. Always needing something. They'll all be fine. I fixed up the house while she was sick. I put money in the savings, and she can work."

"Wow. You're a top-notch human being, Levi," she said.

He chuckled. "I'm not concerned with what anyone thinks of me. I'm concerned with my life. Living it the way I want. With the money that I happened to be smart enough to get my hands on."

"Then why not just leave? If you have the money—"

"I do not have the money!" he shouted, suddenly out of control again. His fist banged the steering wheel, the car swerving as he cursed Wren and Ryan and everyone else who lived in Hidden Cove.

The tirade went on for several minutes, which gave her time to search the back seat for a weapon.

She found nothing. Not even a piece of paper.

"See, this is the problem," he exclaimed, his voice calmer as he regained control. "Your brother—"

"I don't have a brother," she cut in, trying to push his buttons again, get him riled up and focusing on anything other than her. They were on the road that wound through the mountains now. She could tell by the smoothness and the curves. No stoplights. No slowing down. If he drove them off the side of the mountain, they might both die.

She wasn't afraid of death.

She had faced it down too many times to not know it was coming for her. She knew where her future lay, that she would spend eternity with God and with the people she loved.

But she didn't want to die.

She certainly didn't want to be killed by Levi, her body hidden somewhere in the wilderness, everyone she loved and cared about wondering what had happened to her. If she went down, she would go fighting. Other than that, she had no solid plan for escape.

"You know who I'm talking about. Ryan. We were chums in high school. Did you know that?"

"I didn't."

"We got in a lot of trouble together. Only he always took the blame. I always slipped away before anyone realized I was part of it. It worked out well. When he joined the sheriff's department, I thought, why not? And I did the same."

"I'm assuming you two didn't live on the up-and-up while you were working for the sheriff?"

"He did. I got good at taking confiscated narcotics and selling them in the next town over. I had a decent clientele there, was bringing in a good amount of extra money, and then the sheriff got wise to the fact that things were missing. I had to stop for a while. Then my wife got sick, and I decided I needed more than a small-time illegal drug business. Sunrise Acres was just being built. I watched half the older people in town sign up to buy there, and I decided that there had to be a way to get some of the wealthier ones to part with their money. It took a while, but I figured out the perfect solution to my problems. I registered a fake investment company, did everything I had to make it legal, printed up brochures and talked Lester into being my front man."

"You're saying Garner Investment Initiative doesn't own Sunrise Acres?"

"It doesn't own anything. If anyone had bothered to do a thorough investigation, they would have realized that."

"You did a good job of making it look

legit. You certainly had some of our agents fooled."

"Like I said, I'm a member of Mensa. The average person can't outwit me, and I almost never miss details. I know how to make the system work for me, and I did it well. What I didn't anticipate was your brother's guilty conscience. Ryan didn't like the fact that old man Stan had become a liability and had to be removed. As a matter of fact, he threatened to go to the sheriff with what he knew. I threatened to kill Abigail. That little shove down the stairs? That was my warning shot. I thought Ryan and I had an understanding, that we had established I was the one in control, but I still planned to leave town. I figured Ryan would eventually crack, and I didn't plan to be here when it happened."

"You weren't planning to kill him?" she asked.

"Why would I do that? We were old friends. He'd amused me for years. I figured I would leave town and let him take the fall when our clients realized what had happened. And then he betrayed me. I kept the cash from our investors in a safe in the clubhouse. Only I knew the combination. He figured it out and took the money before I could run."

"So you killed him?"

"I was still willing to give him a chance. I asked him to return the cash, and he said it was collateral, that he wanted me to quit the force and admit that I had scammed money out of townspeople. He generously offered to not mention that I had helped Stan on his journey to meet his Maker. I told him I would do it, and then I hired a couple of buddies to make sure I didn't have anything to worry about. The night he died, they were going to follow him after his shift. They had uniforms and a marked police car. I figured the flashing lights would be just enough to make him pull over, but it never came to that. I saw him hanging around the rehab center when we were both supposed to be on patrol. When I realized he was following you home, I knew I had to act. I called my buddies, and they joined me. We saw him pull you over, and I knew he wanted to give you something that might implicate me, so I shot him."

"And you sent your friends to arrest me?"

"They were supposed to kill you and bury your body where no one would find it. Obviously, they did a poor job. They won't repeat that mistake."

"Are they dead?"

He shrugged, the car bouncing over rocky terrain and finally coming to a stop. "We're here," he said. "Let's get this done. I have a new life to begin."

He opened the back door and dragged her out.

The beach was exactly as she remembered it. Rock-speckled sand and seaweed drifting in on brackish waves. There were no people here. No houses. No one to hear her cry out for help. She had a choice—

try to escape now or wait until they were in the cave. There were rocks there, big ones that she and Titus had carried up to make a firepit near the mouth of the cave. They had spent several winter evenings there, feeding the flames and watching the tide roll in.

She had told him that she had loved him once upon a time. She hadn't told him that she still did. She regretted that the same way she regretted not spending more time with Ryan. She had limited her life to her work and to her friends. She had cut herself off from anyone who might hurt her. She had thought she was protecting her heart, but as she walked toward the granite cliff that rose above the beach, she couldn't help wondering if all she had really done was close herself off to possibilities.

"I have a visual." The sheriff's voice carried through the earbud Titus wore, the words filling him with anticipation and relief.

"Both of them?" he whispered into the microphone Radley had pinned to his jacket before he'd rappelled down to the cave. The team that had assembled to save Wren had agreed that walking on the beach might leave visible footprints that would warn Levi away. They had also agreed to send both Titus and Radley down to the cave.

"Both. Looks like she's injured. Plus she's got that broken wrist. I don't know how she's going to make it up to the cave."

"Can you get a clear shot?" Radley broke in. Like Titus, he was at the mouth of the cave, staring down at the beach. They had seen the car arrive, but heavy sleet prevented them from seeing who got out of it. The sheriff and Annalise lay on top of the cliff, using binoculars to track Levi and Wren's progress.

"No. He's behind her. Looks like he has a gun pointed at her back. I'm a good shot, but not a great one. With this sleet and—"

"You don't have to justify the decision,

Sheriff. We're in agreement that it's better to wait." Radley motioned for Titus to move closer. "She'll make it up here. We both know it. She'll be coming up first, leading the way. We don't want to make any noise that will scare him away. We'll wait until they're both here."

"And then what?" he asked, finally spotting the dark figures moving through the sleet toward the cliff.

"You stay out of the way, and I'll take him down."

"That's not a very specific plan."

"It's the best I've got. Levi has already shot and killed two people. It's very possible he tried to murder Hannah and Stan. We have no idea what he is capable of and no way to predict what he might do. That's why I wanted to confront him here. There's less room for him to maneuver his way out of our trap."

And, hopefully, less chance of him hurting Wren.

They had discussed the plan at length.

Trying to intercept Levi on the beach had seemed too risky. He was a crack shot and could easily fire the gun before he was taken down.

This, though, suddenly felt just as risky—the dark cave opening out onto a twenty-foot drop, the wide cavern stretching fifteen feet to the back wall. Someone had once used it as a home. Titus and Wren had discovered it long after that person was gone, but there were niches carved into the walls and an old wooden trunk that had been filled with canned goods. Eventually, he and Wren had emptied it out and put their own treasures inside. Favorite photos and flowers from prom, and a bunch of other things he couldn't remember.

"They're heading up," the sheriff said, his voice tense.

That was Titus's cue to move back, but he wanted to stay where he was, waiting until Wren was within reach and then pulling her up like he had so many times before.

But, if Levi caught a glimpse of him, there was no telling what he would do, and Titus didn't dare risk Wren's life on the chance he wouldn't be seen. They had climbed the cliff in every kind of weather. Sun and snow and wind and calm. They had known every foot-and handhold that had been carved deep into the granite. He thought he could still climb it with his eyes closed.

He hoped the same was true of Wren.

He prayed it was, because there was nothing he could to do help her now but slither to the back of the cave and wait silently for her to arrive.

THIRTEEN

It had been years since she had climbed the cliff, and she had never done it with a broken wrist. Wren stood at the bottom and looked up, sleet falling on her hair and face and melting on her frigid skin. She was cold to the bone, her head throbbing maddeningly. She felt dizzy and off balance standing on the ground. She had no idea how she would feel hanging from rock face.

"Please, God, help me do this," she prayed aloud, knowing it would amuse Levi and not caring. She had to make it up far enough ahead to find a weapon she could use against him.

She could shove him from the cliff as he pulled himself into the cave. That was when he would be most vulnerable, but she wanted him in jail. Not dead.

"God isn't going to help you, Wren," he said with a chuckle that made her hair stand on end. "So you're going to have to help yourself. Here's how I'm going to do it. I'll count to five. If you're still within arm's reach of me when I get to six, I'll kill you here and find my own way up. One."

As she reached for the first handhold, she thought she saw something moving along the ridge above the cliff, but visibility was terrible. It could have been nothing other than a shifting of shadows or a trick of her eyes.

She wanted it to be more. She wanted it to be Radley and Titus and Annalise searching for her. She wanted to believe help had arrived and that she wasn't going to have to fight this battle alone.

"Two," Levi intoned, and she hoisted herself up, stepping into a foothold four feet from the ground.

She needed her left hand for the next section, and she gritted her teeth as she reached for the handhold and pulled herself up. Searing pain ripped through her arm and white-hot light seemed to steal her vision. Breathless, dripping sweat despite the cold, she shifted her weight, moving from one foothold to the next.

"Three."

She thought she was out of his reach, but his fingers tickled the back of her leg, and her stomach heaved.

Don't vomit. Whatever you do, don't do that.

Abigail's voice was echoing through her head. Or maybe it was Titus cheering her on, coaching her up, the way he had done the very first time they had climbed.

"Four."

She reached for the next handhold, another left-handed grip. She couldn't feel her fingers. She had no idea how deep they were in the crevice. She could only move forward on faith, trusting in her hard-earned strength and in God's grace. The pain was duller this time, her clammy reaction to the effort warning her she might be going into shock.

That was fine.

Her body could do whatever it wanted after she stopped Levi.

"Five."

She had reached the mouth of the cave, the fingers of her right hand skimming over the lip and feeling the cool stone floor. She and Titus had spent hours speculating about the impressive cave that had been carved into rock.

They had wondered aloud who had done it, why and with what tools. Those had been good years. When she and Titus had been free to explore the world and to stake their claim on it. She had forgotten how much she loved exploring with him until he had sent her the photo of the old house and she had walked around the pond, palm to palm with him.

She wanted a chance to do that again.

"Six," Levi said as she managed to pull herself over the lip and into the cave.

He chuckled, the maniacal sound echoing through the cave.

He had been behind her the entire time, and he was up and inside the cave before she lifted herself off the stone floor.

"So this is it," he said, his voice too loud for the confined space. This was a place for whispered secrets and quiet conversations, for soft laughter and shared dreams.

It wasn't a place someone like Levi should ever have entered.

"Yes. The trunk is in the back. I'll bring it."

"Trunk?"

"That's where I think Ryan put your money." It was also where she and Titus had stored books and mementos. There was a trophy from her first debate win there. Heavy with a marble base, it might be an efficient weapon.

"We'll go together." He pulled a cell phone from his pocket and turned on the flashlight. She heard something scuffling in the darkness at the back of the cave. Not a bird. They wouldn't have gone so deep into the darkness.

Someone was there.

The thought filled her with hope and with worry. If Levi realized it, he would begin firing random shots into the dark.

"What was that?" he demanded, his gun swinging in the direction of the sound. Away from her but pointed toward some-one.

She was certain of it.

"Bats," she lied.

The gun shifted back in her direction, the light from the phone he held in his left hand shining straight into her eyes.

"There are bats up here?"

"It's a cave. Bats are attracted to them." She resisted the urge to add *Mr. Mensa* at the end. She wanted him distracted from the sound but not angry enough to knock her out again.

"Shut up," he growled, grabbing her

upper arm and shoving her toward the back of the cave. "Get the trunk. Bring it to me."

"Okay," she said, stepping away, her hand skimming the wall to her right. She found the first alcove quickly, grabbed one of the heavy stones she had put there for decoration.

"What are you doing?" he screamed, suddenly right beside her, the gun pressed to her cheek as he screamed into her ear.

"Getting the trunk. Just like you asked me to," she said, and then she gripped the rock and swung her fist at his head with as much strength as she had left.

Levi's roar filled the cave as he fell back, the phone dropping from his hand as he reached for his head. Titus didn't wait for another chance. He lunged from the left side of the cave, tackling Levi as he lifted the gun and fired in Wren's direction. She was on her belly, crawling to the trunk that was pushed up against the back wall.

"No!" Levi screamed, struggling against Titus, his strength seeming nearly super-human.

"I was supposed to handle this part," Radley muttered as he reached down and pulled Levi's arm behind his back, ratcheting up the effort until the gun dropped from his hand.

"You weren't moving fast enough," Titus said, holding Levi's other arm against the ground.

"Let me up," he demanded, twisting and turning as he fought their hold. "There's been some kind of mistake."

"The only mistake we've made was in not realizing what you were from the very beginning," Titus growled.

"You're going to regret this," Levi spit, his eyes wild as he continued to struggle.

"Oh…my," Wren said, her voice shaking. She had the trunk open, and she reached in, the muted light from the facedown phone illuminating her as she pulled out a stack of money bound together with a rubber band.

"That's mine," Levi screamed, bucking away as Radley snapped a cuff on his wrist. It dangled there as he charged toward Wren. "You ruined everything. Just like your brother."

Titus grabbed his shoulder, swinging him away, feeling the razor-sharp sting of a knife blade as Levi swung around, a knife in his hand.

"He's still armed," he shouted, dodging to the left and trying to knock the knife from Levi's hand.

"Stop!" Radley shouted.

"Don't you know you're always supposed to frisk the suspect?" Levi crowed as he ran at Titus.

Titus dodged to the left as Levi darted toward the mouth of the cave.

"I said stop," Radley demanded, and then he raised his service weapon and fired.

Levi fell backward, the knife flying

from his hands and tumbling out of the cave. He landed hard, blood seeping from a wound in his shoulder, curses spilling out of his mouth as he tried to get to his feet.

"Do me a favor. This time, stay down," Radley muttered, flipping him over so he was lying on his stomach, patting his pockets and pant legs, searching for another weapon.

Titus rushed to Wren's side, placing an arm around her waist as she swayed toward him.

"Are you okay?" he asked, concerned by the amount of blood on her face and shirt, the paleness of her face and the wild trembling of her muscles.

"I am now," she claimed, swaying against him, her good arm sliding around his waist.

"You don't look okay," he commented, taking off his coat and wrapping it around her, running his hands up and down her back to try to warm her.

"Gee, thanks, Titus. That's just what every woman wants to hear. You're a pal," she said, her forehead pressed to his chest, her voice muffled by his shirt.

"I'd like to be more than that," he whispered, his lips brushing her ear.

"How much more?" she asked, leaning back and looking into his eyes. She had a deep slash on her cheekbone and a bump on the side of her forehead, and she still was the most beautiful woman he had ever seen.

"As much more as two people can be."

"That's a lot more," she murmured.

"Too much?"

"Just enough," she replied, levering up and planting a gentle kiss on his lips. "When are we going to start?"

"Doing what?"

"Learning to be more than pals?" she asked.

"As soon as you're ready."

"I was ready prom night," she replied,

smiling despite her obvious fatigue and injuries.

"You know what?" he whispered against her lips. "I think I was, too."

She laughed, the sound ringing through the cave and filling his heart with the kind of love he had never imagined he could feel.

"I love you," he said, the truth refusing to remain unspoken.

"I love you, too," she replied. "Now, how about we blow this joint and get started on our happily-ever-after?"

"If you're ready to go," Radley called from the mouth of the cave, still holding Levi down. "Your chariot is waiting."

He gestured to a rappel line and harness that had been lowered to the cave.

"It's not what I was expecting," she joked, taking Titus's hand as she walked toward it.

"No?" he said, helping her into the harness and cinching it for her.

"I had visions of Cinderella's chariot. Sparkling and fancy, being pulled by a bunch of white steeds. But this—" she tugged at the rope, leaning back as she was slowly pulled up "—is so much better."

She blew him a kiss as she disappeared.

He thought he felt it tickle his cheek, whisper across his lips and settle deep into his heart. For the first time in more years than he could remember, he felt like he had finally found his way home.

FOURTEEN

Spring came to Hidden Cove just like it always did. In fits and starts. Storms and sunshine.

By mid-May, flowers had finally appeared in the garden behind Abby's house. The cornfield had been tilled and planted. Soon green shoots would spring up from the rich earth. Wren had spent plenty of time helping at the farm. A severe concussion and twice-broken arm had forced her to take months off work. She had thought she would be occupied prepping for Levi's trial, but he had confessed to his crimes and had been sentenced to life in federal prison. Instead of spending long days with the prosecuting team, Wren had spent time at the hospital, encouraging Hannah as she recovered. She'd spearheaded efforts to make sure the people who had invested in Levi's scheme were repaid. She'd watched the farm spring back to life and helped where she could. She'd kept busy, because that was what she was used to, but she had also found time for the things that were important. Abigail. Friends.

Titus.

And, now, she had finally received the doctor's approval to return to work the first week of June. She and Titus would be back from their honeymoon by then. They planned to split their time between her Boston apartment and his place in Hidden Cove. For now, Abigail was living there with him. Eventually, the farmhouse would be restored, and that would be their main residence. Wren planned to work during the week and travel back to Maine on the weekends. Titus would spend as much time in Boston as he could. It was an unconventional arrangement, but Wren had no doubt they could make it work. She smoothed the skirt of her dress nervously, staring into the full-length mirror in the church's dressing room. She had chosen a simple dress. No fuss or muss. No sequins or sparkle. Just thick white silk that draped her narrow body perfectly.

"I hope he likes it," she said, eyeing her reflection critically. She had never spent much time worrying about her appearance, but today was special. Today was the day she and Titus would commit their lives to one another. She had never imagined it happening. All those years ago, when they had been best friends exploring the world together, she hadn't dared to believe that their bond would grow into a love that would last a lifetime.

"You hope Titus likes your dress? That man would love anything you wore. If you wore burlap, he'd swoon," Annalise said. There were no bridesmaids crowded into the room. No circle of friends ready to stand beside Wren as she said her vows. After so many years apart, she and Titus hadn't wanted to waste time. They loved each other. They knew they wanted to spend their lives together. Those things had seemed as natural as breathing. So, they'd planned the wedding quickly with the support of their friends and family. No attendants, but Annalise had insisted on playing wedding planner, her organized, efficient approach making a close wedding date possible.

"Titus is too masculine to swoon," Abigail cut in, powdering her nose with a powder puff that she pulled from an ornate compact.

"You know what I mean. I've never seen anyone so besotted with another person. If God put someone like that in my life, I would spend every morning on my knees thanking Him for the gift. Every guy I meet isn't worth the cost of gas to go to dinner with him."

"You're too young to be so cynical," Abigail said. "But you're right about Titus. He's a great man, and he loves Wren deeply."

"Yes, he does," Wren agreed, her pulse jumping as she heard the first strains of the "Wedding March" drifting through the intercom. "That's our cue," she said, not moving. Barely breathing.

She felt she had been waiting for this her entire life.

And she was terrified.

Afraid that the trust she had in Titus was misplaced. That she was making the same mistake her mother had. That she would fall asleep in a dream and wake in a nightmare.

"Whatever you're thinking, don't," Abby said, taking her arm and leading her into the hall. The double-wide doors in the sanctuary were closed, two ushers waiting to open them.

"How do you know I'm not thinking something good?" Wren asked nervously, her fingers drifting to the still-purple scar that bisected her cheek.

"Because, I know you. You're terrified. Afraid this is a mistake. Worried he isn't who he seems to be. I'll tell you this. That young man spent hours at my house putting it back to right. He never complained. Never lost his cool. Never raised his voice. If he isn't a keeper, I don't know who is."

"I know you're right," she said. "It's just—"

"You've been hurt, and you're afraid, but sometimes the hurt ends, Wren. Sometimes, we wake one morning, and we see the sunrise and we realize how beautiful it is. We look at the world, and we see the extraordinary in it. And the pain begins to fade, and we begin to live again. That's where you are. Living again. Don't let fear stop you. Rise with your faith in hand, walk through those doors and live like every day is the most extraordinary of miracles."

She was right.

Wren knew it.

She took a deep breath, inhaling the sweet scent of the lilacs she carried. "Right. I'm ready. Let's go."

Annalise hurried to adjust her veil

one last time, then kissed her cheek and stepped aside. "You're going to have the best of lives, Wren. I know it."

"Of course she is." Abby smiled, hooking her arm through Wren's as the ushers opened the doors. The music swept out and into the vestibule, pulling Wren forward into a sanctuary filled with people she knew and loved. Her coworkers and friends. High school teachers who had been both exasperated and encouraging.

Her gaze swept over the crowd of people and landed on the one person who loved her most, the man she loved with every part of her heart.

Titus stood near the pulpit, his suit perfectly fitted, his eyes gleaming ocean blue in the candlelight. When she met his eyes, he smiled, and all her fear fled. All her doubts left.

She moved toward him, Abby hurrying along beside her, beaming with the pleasure of walking her down the aisle.

Titus met them a few feet from the altar.

He took Abby's hand and kissed her cheek. "Thank you," he said.

"She could have made it here all on her own," Abby said, a flush of pleasure staining her cheeks.

"Thank you for parenting two troubled kids who didn't know what it meant to be loved," he continued.

Abby's blush deepened, and Wren was certain there were tears in her eyes. "You always were a charming one, and I always knew the two of you were meant to be. I'm glad you finally both saw the sense in it. Now, take your bride's hand, and let's get this done."

She placed Wren's hand in his, kissed Wren's cheek and then walked to the front pew, taking a seat beside Radley and his wife.

"You are the most stunningly beautiful woman I have ever known," Titus murmured, kissing her knuckles and studying her face.

"And you are the most stunningly beautiful man I have ever known," she replied.

His smile broadened, his eyes sparkling with amusement. "I've never been called stunning or beautiful, but I'll take it. Are you ready to get this thing done?"

"I've been ready…" she replied.

"Since prom night?" he asked.

She smiled, resting her palm against his smooth cheek and looking into his eyes, seeing their past and the future written clearly in his gaze.

"…since the day we met," she responded, and he bent toward her, breaking the rules of etiquette and kissing her tenderly, sweetly. As if they had all the time in the world. As if there was nothing more important than this moment with her.

And maybe there wasn't.

She heard the roar of guest approval, but her heart was bursting for Titus, for the love that had been forged through friendship and that had weathered the test of time.

"I love you," he whispered. "Until there is no breath left in me, I will love you."

"I love you, too. You are the only person I have trusted with every piece of my heart."

He nodded solemnly. "That's the best gift I have ever received."

"And you are the only one I will ever give it to."

"Now let's do this."

"Let's," she agreed, squeezing his hand, letting her smile show all the love she had for him.

They took the last steps to the altar together, hand in hand, shoulder to shoulder, connected in a way that Wren knew would last. Not just for a day or a month or a year. For a lifetime. For all the moments they had left. For the good days and the bad ones and all the days in between. For every disappointment and every triumph, they were committing their hearts to one another.

As the pastor began to speak, Wren

could think of no more beautiful way to celebrate spring than to marry Titus. Every year, when new life sprang from thawing earth and dormant seed, she would remember the way it felt for new love to spring from the dormant seeds of the old.

And she would thank God, always, for finally bringing her back to the only man she had ever loved.

* * * * *

Mistaken Identity
Christmas on the Run

Available now from
Love Inspired Suspense!
Find more great reads at
www.LoveInspired.com

Dear Reader,

No matter how much we plan and plot our lives, we can find ourselves in surprising and oftentimes difficult circumstances. Relationships, health concerns, finances all have a way of weighing on our minds and causing us stress and worry. There are days when it may seem that our fear outweighs our faith, times when we can't see the blessings through the pain. If you've had days when you struggle, times when you feel abandoned and lonely and hurt, if your life is nothing like you expected or planned, remember that you are not alone. God hears your prayers. He understands your pain. He is your ever-present help in troubled times. May you find comfort and hope in the truth of His love for you.

Blessings,

Shirlee McCoy